ALL TIED UP

ABBI GLINES

NEW YORK TIMES BESTSELLING AUTHOR

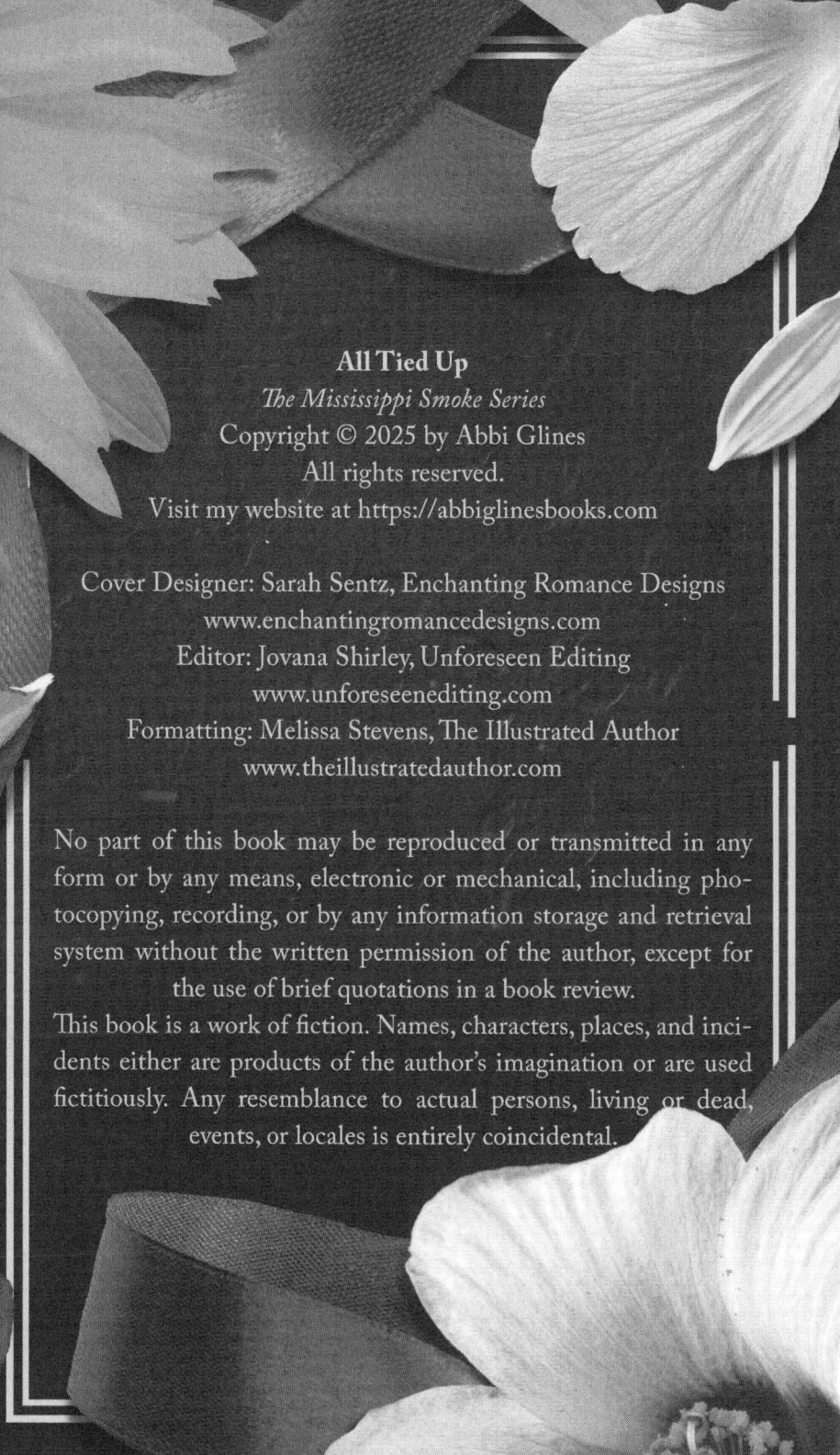

All Tied Up
The Mississippi Smoke Series
Copyright © 2025 by Abbi Glines
All rights reserved.
Visit my website at https://abbiglinesbooks.com

Cover Designer: Sarah Sentz, Enchanting Romance Designs
www.enchantingromancedesigns.com
Editor: Jovana Shirley, Unforeseen Editing
www.unforeseenediting.com
Formatting: Melissa Stevens, The Illustrated Author
www.theillustratedauthor.com

• THE FAMILY •

started by Jediah Hughes. It began with horse racing, moonshine, and illegal arms in the early 1900s

Jediah Hughes

Eustis

Elmer
(died from Typhoid at ten years old)

Feldman

Tipper

Garrett

Gregory
(died at three years old in a house fire)

• THE HUGHES •
Hughes Farm

Garrett Hughes (BOSS in books 1-9)
Wife: **Fawn Parker Hughes** → *SCORCH*

Blaise Hughes (Current BOSS/oldest son)
Wife: **Madeline Walsh Hughes** (parents Etta Marks/dead and Liam

Trev Hughes
Fiancée: **Gypsi Parker** (also stepsister) → *FIRECRACKER*

Cree Elias Hughes → *SMOKESHOW* and *FIREBALL*

• THE SHEPHARDS •

Oldest family inside the southern mafia other than the Hughes

Charles Livingston Shephard
Best friend of Jediah Hughes

Gerald

Joseph
(became a priest)

Jeffrey
(died from Spanish influenza at fifteen years old)

Charles II

Darwin
(died from gunshot at twenty-four)

Charles III
(drowned in childhood)

Joshua
(became a missionary)

Lincoln

Lincoln II (Linc)

Stellan

Mississippi Branch

Linc Shephard
(left Florida to run Mississippi Branch when **Levi** was twenty-two)

Florida Branch

Levi Shephard
Wife: **Aspen Chance Shephard**→ *WHISKEY SMOKE*

Georgia Branch
Shephard Ranch

Stellan Shephard
Wife: **Mandilyn Shephard**

Thatcher
→ *DEMONS*

Sebastian
→ *SMOLDER*

• THE KINGSTONS •
Mars Kingston joined the family in 1921

Mars Kingston
Childhood friend of Jediah Hughes

Hollis

Son
(died in childhood)

Atticus

Son
(died in childhood)

Rollin

Raul

Creed

Barrett

Florida Branch

Creed Kingston (dead)
Wife: **Abigail Kingston** (dead)

Huck
Wife: **Trinity Bennett Kingston**
→ *SMOKE BOMB*

Hayes (dead)
engaged to **Trinity**
at his death

Georgia Branch

Barrett Kingston
Wife: **Annette Kingston**

Storm
→ *SIZZLING*
and *STORM*

Lela
*Book coming in
2025*

Nailyah
*Book coming in
2025*

• THE HOUSTONS •

Joined the family through horse racing in 1938

Kenneth Houston Wife: **Melanie Houston**

|

Saxon Houston
Wife: **Haisley Slate Houston** →
SMOKIN' HOT

|

Winter Noel Houston

• THE LEVINES •
Joined the family in 1977

Alister Levine

|

Mississippi Branch

Luther Levine
Ex-Wife: **Chloe Wall**
(Moved from Florida when **Kye** was nineteen)

|

Florida Branch

Kye Levine
Wife: **Genesis Stoll Levine** → *BURN*

|

Jagger Henley Levine

• THE PRESLEYS •
Joined the family after graduation

Gage Presley
Best friend of Blaise Hughes in high school
Wife: **Shiloh Carmichael Presley** → *STRAIGHT FIRE*

• THE SALAZARS •

Joined the family through horse racing in 1958

Georgia Branch only

Efrain Salazar

Gabriel Salazar (dead)
Wife: **Maeme Salazar**

Ronan Salazar
Wife: **Jupiter Salazar**

King Salazar
→ *SLAY* and
SLAY KING

Birdie
w/Ex Wife: **Estela Salazar**

• THE JONES •
Joined the family through joined real-estate in 1966

Georgia Branch only

Hoyt Jones

Monte
Fiancée: **Bay Mintley**

Roland
Wife: **Luella Jones**

Wilder Jones
Wife: **Oakley Watson Jones** →*ASHES*

Wells Jones
Book date coming soon

Teller Jones
Book coming in 2025

Sarah Jones

• THE RICES •

Oldest family in Mississippi Branch. Hiram Rice left Ocala in 1912 to move to Madison, Mississippi and run a speakeasies in Jackson and one on Madison both Jediah Hughes had purchased. Illegal gambling as well as moonshine was sold inside the bars.

Mississippi Branch

Hiram Rice

Whitmill   **Frances**

Junior

Hart

Gannon (former head of Mississippi Branch. His Parkinson's progressed until he had to step down 12 years ago. Linc Shepherd was moved there to become head over Mississippi Branch)
Wife: **Edy Rice**

Fia Rice Castron   **Saylor**
(married to a member
of Louisiana Branch)

• THE CARVERS •

Awbrey Carver joined the family in 1928 through bootlegging and running illegal gambling rings.

Mississippi Branch only

Awbrey Carver

|

Robert

|

Hale
Wife: **Lethia Carver** (dead)

Ransom   **Opal**   **Than**

• THE CASHES •
The Cash Ranch

Mississippi Branch only

Hawkins Cash
Joined the family in 1922 through horse racing

Samuel
(shot and killed at
20 years old)

William

Fender
Wife: **Grissele Cash**

Bane
→ *TORE UP*

Crosby

• THE SAVELLES •
Savelle Stables

Mississippi Branch
Oz Savelle
joined the Family in 1967 through horse

|

Jonas
Wife: Ellender Savelle

Oz   Forge   Kash

Alabama Branch
Kash Savelle
moved to Alabama Branch when he turned 21

• THE BOWENS •
Lewis Bowen joined the family in 1975

Mississippi Branch
Lewis Bowen
Oz Savelle's best friend since childhood

Malbrough 'Mal"
Ex-Wife: **Celeste**

Locke   **Gathe**

ACKNOWLEDGMENTS

This one took me all summer. I'm a fast writer normally but this summer was busy. I'm thankful for the memories I made with those I love but it felt good to finally get back behind the desk and delve into the world of my southern mafia men. I'm asked often how I pull off a book a month and I have one answer for that... THESE people are how I do it:

Britt is always the first I mention because without him, our house might literally fall apart.

Emerson for surviving without me. I would say she didn't complain but that would be a lie. There is always a lot of standing at my office door and scowling at me.

My older children, who live in other states, they called and texted and were also ignored. I felt bad but I replied "Writing, deadline, will call when finished." And they didn't mind but they also didn't stop calling and texting so... anyway. Thankfully my second granddaughter has waited until after I finished the edits on this one before making her appearance. I am ready for her now. She can hurry it on along. God knows her momma is ready too.

My editor, Jovana Shirley at Unforeseen Editing. She worked with my tight schedule, and I would be screwed without her. She's a God send. (this seems to be happening monthly so I might as well copy and paste this with each Acknowledgments section) I need to start sending her wine baskets every month for putting up with me.

My formatter, Melissa Stevens at The Illustrated Author. Who has never let me down. She always does a speedy turn around for me (monthly I might add). She makes my books beautiful inside. Her work is the best formatting I've ever had in my books. She works with my tight schedule, the deadlines I miss and always makes sure I have an excellent finished product.

Autumn Gantz, at Wordsmith Publicity, for saving me from losing my mind and taking over all the things that I can't keep up with anymore. Her help allows me to write this quickly. She reminds me of the things I need to do. I don't think I would have been able to keep up with this one book a month schedule without her.

Beta readers, who come through every time: Jerilyn Martinez, and Vicci Kaighan. I love y'all!

Sarah Sentz, Enchanting Romance Designs, for my book cover. Again, she nailed it. I have no visual creativity to give her any help in the matter. But she manages to create something I adore every time.

Abbi's Army, for being my support and cheering me on. I love y'all!

My readers, for allowing me to write books. Without you, this wouldn't be possible.

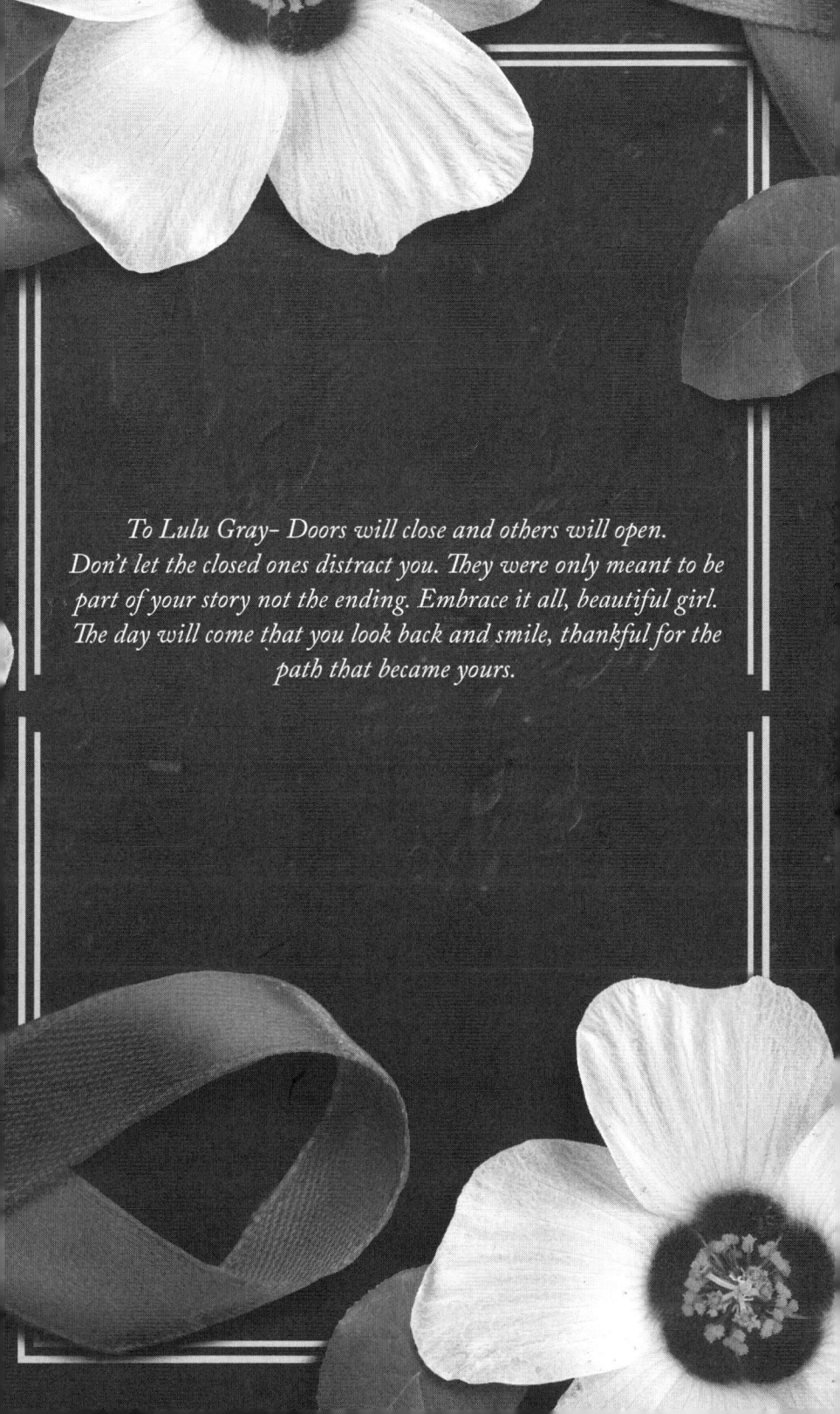

To Lulu Gray– Doors will close and others will open. Don't let the closed ones distract you. They were only meant to be part of your story not the ending. Embrace it all, beautiful girl. The day will come that you look back and smile, thankful for the path that became yours.

ONE

NOA

My eyes swung from the security camera at the entrance to my building complex back to my bedroom. The sound of running water reminding me that Ransom Carver was in my shower. That still seemed unreal. The bubble of excitement at the thought was burst quickly, when the front entrance buzzed again.

Frowning, I stared at Thurston on the screen. Why was he here? I hadn't given him my address. I would have to blame that on my best friend, Jellie. She meant well, but there was no spark with Thurston.

While there was a raging fire with Ransom. One I was afraid was going to burn me to the ground, but I wasn't about to tread carefully.

Ransom had shown up in my apartment last night and said things that I never thought I'd hear him say. Then there had been a lot of sex. I smiled, biting my lip and thinking about what all we'd done.

Thurston sighed heavily and pulled out his phone to begin what looked like texting. I bit down too hard on my lower lip, unsure of what to do, then let it go with a wince. He hadn't texted or called me first. We'd just met this weekend. Shouldn't he have at least sent me a text before showing up here? And why was he already back from Boston? What about his car?

I'd forgotten about that already—well, until now. Although it had just been yesterday morning, it felt as if more time had passed. Ransom had a way of distracting me. He always had. Even when it was just his words I read on my phone.

Deciding that ignoring Thurston would make things weird and he'd probably start calling, I pressed the button that unlocked the door for him to enter, then ran a hand through my tousled hair. Not that I was trying to look good for Thurston, but I didn't want to answer the door with a *just been fucked* look. I doubted Ransom would want that either.

I stared hard at the door, wondering if I'd made a mistake. Maybe I should have ignored him and dealt with this later. I wasn't positive if I even had anything to deal with at all. Ransom had said things about not sharing me. The memory sent a warm surge of joy through my chest. One that I would probably regret later.

Facing a future heartbreak was a price I was willing to pay if it meant I got Ransom. Even for a little while. The fear that I could lose him and our friendship was annoyingly there in the back of my mind, but it didn't have much time to bloom before the knock on my door interrupted it.

Crap. I should have just ignored this. I could have sent Thurston's call to voicemail and dealt with it later.

Sighing, I unlocked the door and opened it up. Dressed in a pair of freshly pressed khakis and a polo shirt that matched his sea-green eyes stood Thurston Coburg. I refused to call him Thurst, like Jellie's boyfriend, Zeke, did.

His eyes did a quick sweep of my body, which was currently wrapped in a knee-length pink satin robe. I should have put on clothes, but too late for that now.

"Did I wake you up?" he asked as his blond brows drew together in a frown.

While it sure appeared that way, it was also almost eleven. I could see where his confusion might come from.

I shook my head. "No. Just a lazy morning," I replied, which was a lie. Nothing about the past two hours I'd spent with Ransom was lazy.

He gave me a crooked grin at that response, then stepped forward, as if to come inside. That wasn't a great idea, but before I could think of a reason for him not to, he walked past me and into the entryway. I began to panic when his gaze swept the area, as if he was inspecting it. That annoyed me, but I was too busy trying to decide how to get rid of him.

"Nice place. I looked at this complex before I leased the flat I'm at now, but it was a touch too steep for me. Smut novels must be profitable."

Eh, okay, he was starting to piss me off. The tone in his voice, as if what I wrote amused him, was one I was familiar with. It was often one I heard when I was asked about my "smut writing" or something equally insulting. I wrote romance novels. My books had plot. They weren't just porn. Sex was a minor role in the storyline. There was angst, pain, drama, all wrapped up in a pretty bow.

"You could say that," I replied, not trying to mask my dislike of the word smut. Although he didn't seem to pick up on it.

Turning back to look at me, he flashed his perfect white smile that I would bet money was fake.

Thurston walked farther into my apartment, and I followed him, not liking that he was so comfortable making himself at home. He stopped when he came to the large, open kitchen that spread into the living area.

"We never got our brunch. I thought I'd take you to my favorite brunch spot in the city. They have these cutesy mimosa flights I've personally never ordered, but I figured you'd like them."

Because I was a female? I honestly didn't care for mimosas. Champagne wasn't my favorite, but I'd drink it if that was all that was available. If I was going to drink before noon, it would be a Bloody Mary.

"You look like a mimosa guy."

The deep, familiar drawl had my gaze swinging back toward the bedroom door to see Ransom striding out into the hallway in nothing but a towel wrapped around his lower portion. The sight of his messy, damp locks and muscular, defined chest, scattered with tattoos on full display, zapped all other thoughts from my head.

He was beautiful. I'd seen him naked several times now, but the impact of the sight didn't seem to diminish. It might even be growing in strength.

"I, uh, didn't know you had company."

Thurston's words snapped me out of my lust haze, and I turned my attention back to him.

"You didn't give me a chance to tell you," I pointed out.

He'd walked in, uninvited, after all, then continued to talk.

His entire body was now tense, and the displeased look on his face made it clear he wasn't happy about it. I didn't feel bad about this. We'd only met this weekend, and there had been zero sparks. I hadn't planned on seeing him again.

"Go to the bedroom." Ransom's words verged on sounding like a command.

I narrowed my eyes as I met his gaze. "Excuse me?"

The corner of his very talented mouth quirked, as if he was trying not to smile at my reaction to his order. He had really good lips. No, he had excellent lips. My thoughts began to drift back to the things he'd done with them earlier.

"The bedroom, Shakespeare. Take your sweet ass back to it."

Oh, right! He was telling me what to do. My eyes lifted back to his.

"I'm fine right here, thank you," I clipped—or tried to. My voice wavered a little.

He walked past both of us and went to the refrigerator. I watched him silently as he took out a bottle of water, opened it, and took a long drink while his eyes locked on me again.

"Is this a one-night-stand thing? Some pickup at a bar?" Thurston asked, and I was reminded again that he was still here.

Right. I had to fix that.

Shaking my head, I sighed and tore my gaze off Ransom to look at the other man. "No. We're, uh, old friends."

What else did I call him? This was all awkward.

"Then what is—"

"You can go," Ransom replied in a bored tone, cutting off whatever Thurston was about to say.

"Ransom," I scolded him. There was no reason to be rude.

He cocked one eyebrow at me, as if waiting for me to explain myself. I blew out a frustrated breath, then turned my attention back to Thurston, who appeared to be ready for a fight. He should probably be very careful what he said to Ransom. Although I couldn't imagine Ransom doing anything to him, there was that Mafia thing, and I really wasn't positive what it all meant. He had an artillery in his truck alone, and I'd noticed the gun he took off last night and placed on my nightstand. He hadn't tried to hide it.

"You've got five seconds to get in your bedroom before I haul you in there myself." The threat in Ransom's voice sent a shiver through me that meant I must be whacked in the head.

"Let me walk Thurston to the door," I said tightly, cutting my eyes at Ransom.

"No." His short reply sounded final.

His domineering attitude had been a turn-on when we were in the bedroom, but right now, I was getting angry.

"I don't recall asking for permission," I replied, straightening my shoulders and lifting my chin a little higher as I stared him down.

"It sounds as if you might be the one who needs to leave," Thurston said.

Dread pooled in my stomach. *Bad idea, dude. Really bad idea.*

Ransom set his bottle of water down on the counter slowly as his eyes turned cold. His complete focus was now on Thurston. The temperature in the room felt as if it had literally dropped twenty degrees instantly. The sound of my heart racing became a thunder in my ears, and I knew I had to do something to get Thurston out of here.

The deep chuckle that came from Ransom's chest wasn't one that sounded amused at all. A tremor of fear ran through me, and I was frozen.

"Is that what it sounds like?" he asked Thurston in a calculating tone.

The need to wrap my arms over my chest in some form of protection was hard to ignore, but I did. I had to cool him off. The violent glint in his eyes didn't match his smirk. I hoped Thurston read this correctly and ran like hell.

6

"I, uh … well, yes, it does. You're being rude, and you're a guest here." Thurston's voice gave away his uneasiness. He'd read the danger, but he apparently wasn't smart enough to flee from it.

"Come here, Noa." Ransom rarely used my real name.

My feet moved of their own accord. I was closing the short distance between us without hesitation. It was as if I'd written my own actions in a novel. Where was my backbone? Since when did I do as told? Yet with Ransom holding out a hand to me, I knew I didn't have the power to stop myself. I wanted to be close to him.

When I was inches away, he pulled me to his side and draped his arm over my shoulders. The warmth of his breath tickled my ear as he leaned down close to me.

"Tell him who needs to leave," he said in a quiet tone but one that Thurston could easily hear.

I swallowed nervously. He was right. Thurston needed to leave, but this was not the right way to do it. Yet it seemed this was the only way to get the man out safely.

"Ransom is in town for a visit," I told him. "It is best that you go."

Thurston's gaze was on Ransom's arm over my shoulders. His Adam's apple bobbed in his throat.

"It's best that you don't come back," Ransom added in a lazy drawl that still managed to hold a lethal warning.

"I was unaware you were seeing someone," Thurston said, straightening his shoulders.

"Well, now you know," Ransom said and pressed a kiss to my temple.

Oh good Lord, he was laying it on thick.

Thurston appeared as if he would say more, but when he began striding toward the exit, I sagged in relief. A chuckle vibrated Ransom's chest. Tilting my head back, I did my best to glare at him.

He winked at me, which made my chest flutter like the fool I was.

I started to step away. "I should go see him out—"

Ransom's hand clamped down on my hip, where it had slid when I moved. "If you care if he lives, you'll stay put."

A surprised laugh bubbled out of me. "That's a bit dramatic."

His gaze drifted down over my face to my collarbone, then lower. "I believe I mentioned that I don't share," he said as he ran a fingertip over the slight gap in the top of my robe. "I also don't like another man seeing you dressed like this."

I started to point out that I was covered up when his hand slid inside and cupped one of my bare breasts, then squeezed so hard that I yelped.

"Don't let it happen again." His voice took on a darker sound, and I shivered. "I can't promise you I won't kill the next fucker who gets this view."

Breathe. It was hard to breathe.

My body was tingling in areas with anticipation while my head was screaming, *Danger. Run.*

I was torn between pressing against him and tearing myself away.

Reaching up, he cupped the side of my face, and his eyes narrowed slightly. "I see fear," he said, studying me. "You should know better than that, Shakespeare. I'd never hurt you."

There was fear, but not for me exactly. More for what I didn't know. How sane was Ransom Carver? Ten years of texting him didn't mean I knew him. I knew only what he'd allowed me to know. What was he not showing me? The glimpse I'd just gotten made me wonder if that was a question I never wanted the answer to.

"You just did," I replied just above a whisper. "Hurt me."

The corner of his mouth tugged in amusement. "Did I squeeze too hard?" he asked, moving in closer to me as he pulled at the belt on my robe until it fell away and left me exposed. "Let me kiss it and make it better," he said, caressing my left breast as he lowered his head to press his lips to the curve of my jawline. "And then I'll move between your sweet thighs and kiss there too."

My knees buckled slightly, and I grabbed on to his arms to steady myself. All other concerns seemed to melt away. Leaving me needy and very, very stupid.

The heavy thud of my door closing made me jump. Ransom's eyes shot over my head toward the sound, and a dark scowl came over his face. Wanting to explain Thurston since he'd not asked before ordering me to the bedroom, I squeezed his arms that I still had a grip on to get his attention.

"He is Jellie's boyfriend's best friend. The guy I was set up with this weekend. You know I'm not interested in him."

When he dropped his gaze back to me, it softened. "He seems to feel differently about you."

What did I say to that? It would seem so. But I didn't care. Would that calm him down? I should have never allowed Thurston into the building. This had caused an issue I hadn't anticipated.

"Or he just needs a friend," I replied, deciding that was the best reason.

"Don't be naive, Shakespeare," he told me as he ran a finger over my jawline and down my neck. "You know that's not why he wants to take you to brunch. How many times have I told you that men think with their dicks?"

A small giggle escaped my lips, and I shrugged. "About a million, I'd guess."

"And yet it still hasn't sunk in."

I inhaled deeply, then let it out. "So, is that what this is? What we're doing? You're thinking with your dick?"

His lips quirked, and his eyes followed the trail of his finger as he ran it over my sensitive skin. "Yes, and no." When his eyes shot back up to mine, he asked, "Does it matter?"

Yes, it did. But I wasn't ready to push that. I wanted to have Ransom in my life regardless of the outcome from our sexual activities.

"I guess it doesn't right now." But it would eventually.

"You're thinking about this too hard, Shakespeare. It's time I distracted you."

I wouldn't argue with that.

"But I should feed you first. You need to keep your energy up." He pressed a kiss to the tip of my nose, then glanced around the kitchen. "It's too damn clean to cook in here. Let's order out. I'd prefer to keep you to myself before I have to leave."

Leave. Right. Back to Mississippi. That thought dampened my mood.

He'd be a text and phone call away soon. Not here with me. He could be with any female he chose. Doing whatever he wanted. I'd be here … pining away, missing him, worrying over him being with some other woman.

"Food shouldn't cause such a sad look in those pretty gray eyes."

I did my best to smile and cover up my thoughts. "Just thinking about you leaving, is all," I replied.

He smirked then. "You missing me already?"

Might as well be honest. "Yep. It appears I am."

"Let's order some food, and we can talk."

That sounded slightly unnerving. What would we talk about? This? Us? Was I ready for that? He'd said a lot of things already, but that was when we were about to have sex. Emotions had been high. This was the aftermath. I might not be ready for the *real* just yet.

TWO
RANSOM

> Linc: Bane caught a fucking PI snooping around in town. Asking about YOU. I need motherfucking answers. Get your ass back here. Now!

> Dad: Get home. Whatever shit you pulled wasn't handled properly. You left loose ends.

I sat up in bed with my phone gripped tightly in my hand and glanced down at Noa. Her golden hair fanned over the pillow. Damn, she looked like an angel. One I'd defiled many times in the past twenty-four hours. I wasn't ready to leave her, but would I ever be? At the moment, that seemed to be unlikely.

Standing up, I walked over to my discarded jeans and began dressing. I'd missed two calls from Linc, one from my dad, and three from Bane. His were first. He had probably

12

tried to warn me about this shit. I'd broken a rule and put my phone on silent. My selfishness to have Noa with no interruptions had led to missing calls I shouldn't have. Yet I didn't seem to care. I might change my mind when I got back to Madison and had to face Linc's angry ass.

Once I had my shirt on and my gun tucked away in its holster, I walked over to her side of the bed. Reaching down, I brushed a lock of hair from her face. I didn't want to go. I needed more time here. With her. We'd failed to define anything, but that was my doing. I hadn't wanted to label us. Leaving her without some claim on her made me uneasy, but then the way she had looked at me last night when I emptied my load inside her looked like she was claimed with or without the words.

The fluttering of her lashes came just before she stared up at me.

"I gotta go," I told her in a raspy tone from sleep.

She frowned, then pulled herself up to a sitting position, and not looking at her bare tits before she covered them with the sheet was impossible. Fuck, I didn't want to go.

"What's wrong?" Her voice sounded husky and sexy as hell.

"Some shit back home. They blew up my phone. I've been summoned back." And I feared it might have to do with the missing jackass she'd been engaged to.

She ran a hand through her messy strands, and a flicker of anxiety crossed her face.

I reached down and cupped her chin. "It's all good. Go back to sleep. I'll call you later this morning. After the sun has come up."

She sighed, then nodded.

I fought the desire to kiss her. If I did, there was a good chance I wouldn't stop there. I was already in trouble. I didn't need to make it worse. Linc, when he'd been angered, was never easy to deal with.

My phone began to vibrate in my pocket, and I bit back a curse. I had to go. The fact that it was three in the morning, and they were awake, trying to get me on the phone, wasn't good. Stepping away from her so that I couldn't continue to touch her, I tried to smile.

"Go back to sleep," I told her, then turned to walk away.

The more I looked at her, the harder this would be. I hated fucking New York City, and I hated that she lived here. I wanted her closer. Somewhere I could get to her easily when I needed her. The texting her when shit was dark would no longer do the trick. Not when I knew what it was like to have her naked body in my arms. I much preferred that distraction.

Closing her bedroom door behind me, I pulled out my phone to see Bane had called, and so had my father. Damn, they were acting like this was the fucking Feds. It was a PI. Most likely one hired by the parents of Arden Neilson—Noa's former editor and fiancé. Which meant the religious little farming family still refused to believe Arden's reasons for "skipping town." It also meant the PI wasn't high pro-file. They couldn't afford shit like that—I knew. I'd done my research.

> Bane: I can see you read my fucking text. Answer your phone.

Rolling my eyes, I opened the door to her apartment and stepped out before hitting the Call button.

Making sure the door locked behind me, I only heard the first ring before Bane snapped in my ear, "What the fuck are you doing?"

"Good morning to you too," I drawled.

I knew when he was ready—or rather, when the boss was ready—Linc would hand over the head of the Mississippi branch to Bane. But right now, he wasn't in charge. He could suck a dick. I owed him no explanations.

"Maybe where you are," he replied, annoyed. "That's about to change. Who the hell is Arden Neilson, and what did you do with him?"

Just as I'd guessed. Damn nosy-ass parents of his were causing trouble. I'd prepared for this just in case.

"Editor at a publishing house who was going to be working with Opal. He was shady as hell. Had a fiancée he was cheating on with Opal and she had no idea. I made him go away. She's got a much better editor now," I told him as the elevator opened and I stepped inside.

I left out that Noa had made sure to get Opal an excellent editor. I didn't need to involve Noa in any of this. Using Opal as an excuse would give me just cause in the family's eyes. I knew that, and I worked with it.

Bane blew out a sigh. "Why didn't you tell someone? You don't make the call on shit like that without talking to Linc."

"My sister, Bane. I didn't need Linc's permission."

"Regardless, he's fucking pissed. This might ease it some, seeing as this had to do with Opal, but the PI knows some shit that he shouldn't. You were sloppy as fuck. Not like you. Where was your head?"

Scowling, I stared at the elevator doors. "How was I sloppy?"

"The PI knows who we are. He also keeps saying shit about some fiancée of Neilson's. You've been seen going in and out of her apartment building. He never mentioned Opal in all this."

I'd been trailed and not sensed it! Jesus. Maybe I had been more distracted with Noa than I'd realized.

When the doors opened on the ground floor, my gaze swung over to the security guard who stood at his desk in the lobby. I didn't like knowing some fucking PI had been watching this place. I also didn't like the idea of the Ken Doll showing back up in hopes of taking Noa to brunch.

"I'm headed back now. I'll handle this when I get there," I told Bane.

"You'll be doing more than that. You've caused an issue that isn't going to be easily cleaned up."

Damn, they were being dramatic about this.

He ended the call without waiting for a response while I walked over to the security guard. I'd decided he and I were about to become friends. Especially when I offered him double whatever he was currently getting paid. If I couldn't be here full-time, then I needed other eyes on Noa. Staying focused on anything else would be impossible otherwise.

Once I had this under control, I was going to find a way to get her back to Madison. Fuck this place.

THREE
RANSOM

It was never enjoyable, stepping into Linc Shephard's office. It was worse when my father was also waiting inside, along with Fender Cash. At least Luther Levine was lounging on the sofa, looking more amused than anything. He would be less pissed than the others. God knew he'd done worse.

"About fucking time," my dad said as he glared at me over the rim of his whiskey glass.

"The jet only goes so fast," I replied.

Linc's cold expression made it clear he wasn't amused. Shocker.

"Start at the beginning and don't leave out a goddamn detail," Linc said through clenched teeth as he sat down in the chair behind his desk.

Every detail? Was that necessary? I doubted it.

"I stopped in to see Opal when I took the last load of whiskey to DC for Dad. She had a dinner planned with her new editor at the publishing house that had her book. I went with her. The editor was Neilson. He was shady—engaged

17

and hiding it from Opal, who seemed interested in him. He continued to lie throughout the meal. I did a background check. He had done the same thing with another author a few years ago and she was now his fiancé. I knew Opal wouldn't listen to me, she'd fallen for his charming act bullshit. I didn't want her hurt. So, I handed him over to the cartel. Got us some goodwill with them. A future favor for trading a douchebag for one of their men with some dealings that had gone bad." I shrugged and hoped like fuck this would be enough. "I didn't kill the lying, cheating bastard. I just sold him."

"To the narcos." Luther chuckled, which was better than the other three, who were studying me as if they could read all the shit I had left out. "Nice try, but they already know about the pussy. Might as well fess up to that shit," Luther added, then lit the end of the cigar he'd placed between his teeth.

"Open the fucking window and go stand beside it if you're gonna smoke," Linc ordered.

Luther rolled his eyes and stood up slowly. "This rule sucks ass. A little cigar smoke isn't going to hurt Stevie."

At least the deadly warning in Linc's gaze was now on Luther and not me. Stevie was his six-year-old daughter. His wife was also pregnant with kid number two. He'd banned all smoking in the house when he moved Stevie in, although half of the sprawling mansion belonged to Luther.

Linc swung his gaze back to me. "And Noa Raines? The fiancée? She had nothing to do with your need to get rid of Arden Neilson?"

Fuck. Who the hell had told him about Noa? Probably Gathe. He talked too damn much.

"What about Noa," I clipped out. I was going to plant my fist in Gathe's pretty-boy face.

18

"You've known her for ten years. Texted with her. Kept in contact. Brought her to Bane's house. Let her stay there."

I nodded my head once, waiting to let him tell me what he knew. I wasn't going to elaborate.

"Is this about fucking? Because the last time I checked, you weren't real territorial about the ass you tapped," my dad said, frowning at me like I'd lost my mind.

Maybe I had. It felt like it a little. I'd admit that.

"No, it's not about fucking."

Noa was more than that. She'd been more for longer than a decade. However, the fucking was addictive and seemed to have a hold on me.

"Oh, it's about the fucking. You handed a man over to the narcos to get rid of him. Must be some prime pussy," Luther drawled.

I took a step in his direction, my hands fisted at my sides, before I realized what I was doing. Rage seethed through me, threatening to take over my actions, even when my head was screaming at me to calm the fuck down. They were watching me. I was giving myself away.

Luther's amused laughter was like gas to the flame. "Two down, Hale. Damn, I didn't see this son being the next to get all tied up over a woman. Than was an easy guess, but Ransom?" He shook his head as if he were disappointed in me.

"Arden Neilson's parents have hired one of the best PIs in New York. They're desperate and determined to find their son. Because of your rash decision, we now have that PI in Madison. He's currently in his hotel room, scared to come out. Bane handled that. And we're watching his every move. But he's a dog with a bone and our fucking problem," Linc said.

"He's my problem. I'll go handle him," I told him.

19

"You gonna send him off to the border too?" Luther asked.

Linc shot Luther an annoyed glance. "I don't need your commentary."

"He is sniffing around family property. Asking questions about us. That makes it our problem," my dad said, setting his empty glass down with enough force that it shook the table beside him. "Blaise knows."

Those two words were said calmer, but with a warning that sent a chill down my spine. Blaise Hughes was the boss of the family. All of the family. Every branch of the Southern Mafia answered to him. Although he was in his early thirties, he terrified every man in this room. Even Linc, who had grown up with his father and been there the day he was born.

"How does he want it handled?" I asked with hesitancy. Not sure I wanted this answer.

"Cleaned up. He wants the PI to go away without feeding him to the hogs. And"—Linc leaned forward, resting his elbows on the desk in front of him—"he wants you to stay the fuck away from Manhattan and the blonde writer. No contact."

I felt the blood drain from my face as his words slowly sank in.

I didn't realize I was shaking my head until my father's loud, "YES!" jerked my attention off Linc to him.

"You WILL stay away from the woman. It's an order, Ransom, and in this family, we obey the goddamn orders. No piece of ass is worth disobeying the boss. If it were Garrett, then I'd consider talking with him about it if she meant something to you, but this isn't Garrett. This is Blaise, and where his father could be reasonable, he is not. Do you need a reminder of what happened to Six last year?"

I swallowed hard. No, I didn't want to rehash how one of his men in Ocala, where the family had begun and kept the main headquarters, disobeyed a command. We had all heard about it. Knew he'd paid for it with his life. But Six's mistake had put Blaise's wife and oldest son in danger. When they were involved, Blaise Hughes became the damn Grim Reaper to anyone who got in his path.

"My seeing Noa doesn't put Blaise's family in danger," I pointed out, grasping for a reasonable argument.

Linc shot up from his seat and planted both his hands on the desk as he glared at me. "That doesn't fucking matter!" he roared. "You caused this. YOU chose to act without his command. This is the price you pay. Disobey him, and it'll be your life next. If you mess up his Thanksgiving with this shit, he won't be forgiving. His wife loves the holidays, and he will kill any bastard who threatens to fuck with her happiness. If he has to deal with this shitstorm you made this week or the weeks between now and Christmas, he will put a goddamn bullet between your eyes."

"Blaise lacks morals that his father had. At least where human life is concerned. He's more feared because of it. If you want to keep this *Noa* safe, then you need to do as he says. He's killed women before." My father's words left a ringing in my ears that bordered on painful.

"Ah, come on, Hale. That's a little harsh. Gina deserved what she got. The bitch was crazy as fuck and had handed over his wife to an MC and then kidnapped Levi's woman," Luther said as he leaned against the open window with the cigar between his teeth.

"And if Noa Raines finds out where her fiancé went and who is responsible, do you think she'll be okay with that? No! Blaise will make sure she never gets the chance to talk," my father told Luther angrily.

Luther shrugged. "Maybe."

21

Maybe? Fuck. I couldn't allow Blaise Hughes or his orders anywhere near Noa. This wasn't something I'd even considered when I got rid of Arden. FUCK!

I shoved my fingers into my hair and tried to calm my breathing. The sound of my heart hammering in my chest was so damn loud that it was a wonder it wasn't echoing off the walls in the room. What had I done? I wanted to keep Noa safe. Protect her. But I'd fucking led the devil to her door.

"Bane is waiting to take the PI from his room and bring him to the underground," Fender said, speaking for the first time instead of his silent, judgmental stance. "He's to be silenced, then sent back to the hole he came out of."

Linc glanced at Fender, then back to me. "You'll go with Oz and Locke to help with that. Then, you're to report back here. To me. I'll give you a new cell phone, as you will be leaving the one you have here. No contact with the woman. It's not a suggestion. It's a fucking command."

My teeth clenched as tightly as my fists. "You're saying I can't even text her?" I asked.

"No contact," he replied sternly.

"But—"

"NO CONTACT, SON!" my father shouted.

I swung my glare to him and met his. "Why can't I even text her?!"

"Because you sold her fiancé to the damn cartel and now we have shit to clean up," he replied.

"Lots of pussy in the sea. Don't get so worked up over one." Luther's tone annoyed me.

Normally, I was amused by him, but right now, I wanted to shove his head through the glass of the window, along with the others in the room.

"I don't even get to explain?" I asked Linc.

He shook his head. "No."

A heavy, sick feeling sank over me, making it hard to breathe.

"If we have to lock you up until this is over in order to keep you alive, we will," my father warned.

"Be smart," Fender added.

Be smart? They could all go to hell.

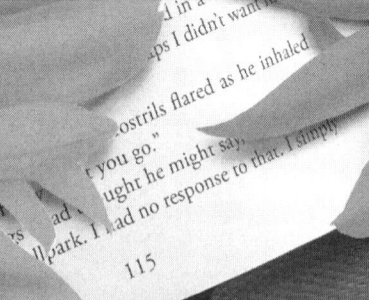

115

FOUR
NOA

Three Days Since Ransom Left …

Folding another piece of clothing into my packing cube, I glanced over at my phone anxiously. I had the ringer on and the volume as high as it would go, so I knew I hadn't missed a call or text, but still … it had been three days. And nothing. Not one text. Not one call. Not even a response to the three texts I had sent him.

The last text I'd sent was yesterday.

> Me: Did you know only male turkeys gobble?

Not only did he not respond, but he also didn't bother to read it. I had stopped after that one. There was a measure of pride that wasn't allowing me to send another. Either he'd turned the Send Read Receipt off in his Settings or he was ignoring my texts altogether.

Sure, we'd gone a week without texting in the past, but he never ignored my text. And that was before … things changed with us. Before we had something more than a back-and-forth on our phones. I had thought this week, he'd send me something. Maybe even a, *What are your Thanksgiving Day plans?* I didn't know … anything.

My mother's death wouldn't affect my holiday. I'd not spent this week with her since I had gone to college. I always went to Jellie's family gatherings. Although this year, I wasn't looking forward to it. She'd see right through me.

Staring at my phone, I realized this was the loudest silence in the world. Every second that ticked by reminded me that he had walked out in the middle of the night, not even kissed me goodbye, and there had been no contact since.

Had he gotten what he wanted and was done? I felt sick at that thought.

Was I that naive? Had I truly read his intentions wrong? Or had he simply woken up the other night, looked at me, and decided he was already bored with me? That was the one thing that seemed to taunt me the most. He had warned me for years that men liked variety and grew bored with one cunt. His words, not mine. Why had I believed mine was any different than the last female he'd been with?

Because I wanted him to want me the way I did him. I wanted him to feel a fraction of what I felt for him. God, how stupid was I? Why couldn't I feel this with a man who wanted one woman?

The house, two kids, a dog, and big back porch overlooking a lush backyard weren't things Ransom Carver wanted in life. That was my ideal. My dream. The life I'd not had, growing up. The love and security of a home that I'd longed for as a child still held power over me.

Going and falling in love with a man who would never—

Wait.

I'd just said *love*.

The shirt in my hand fell from my fingertips, and I stared at the wall. The ache in my chest that had settled with the silence of Ransom cracked a little more. I sucked in a breath as tears stung my eyes.

"Oh God," I whispered.

I shook my head. "No. No, I can't love him. He doesn't want me. He doesn't want a house, kids, a big back porch. He's also dangerous. He has guns."

Turning, I sank down on the bed beside my open suitcase. Saying the words, pointing out the reasons why I couldn't love him, wasn't helping at all. It didn't change anything. The agony expanding and slithering through every fiber of my body was more powerful than any other heartbreak I'd experienced.

"So, this is it," I said to no one.

I'd never felt this. Which meant, until Ransom, I had never been in love. What I'd felt for Arden didn't even scratch the surface of this. He'd been a disappointment, but my chest, my heart, it never suffered.

I placed a hand over the tortured organ and tried to take a deep breath. I had gone and fallen in love with a man who would never feel the same. It put a dark cloud over everything. Zapped my joy completely. Even in the little things, like Thanksgiving at the Wattses' house in Portsmouth, New Hampshire. The thought of waking up to a waffle bar, then watching the Macy's Thanksgiving Day Parade in my pajamas with Jellie on the sofa while her father made comments about the performers from his recliner didn't even lighten my mood. It would often snow that weekend—sometimes the first snow of the season. It always felt magical. Melinda would have Jellie play "Jingle Bells" on the piano and have us all sing along. I'd learned from her that it had originally been written as a Thanksgiving song, but over time, it became a Christmas one. Even Jellie's older brothers, Finton and Birch, would sing along. I normally looked forward to that day all month. I'd barely thought of it this month. All my brain had room for was Ransom, it seemed.

He would eventually text me back. I was almost a hundred percent sure of it. But he was making sure I understood that our having sex hadn't changed the way he felt about me. I wasn't going to become someone he needed to talk to daily. His work was first, and when he had time, he'd get back to me. Maybe he was reinforcing that by leaving my text unread. It was a shitty thing to do. He could have at least responded with a, *Made it back. Busy with work.* Which the week before Thanksgiving week was normally their slammed one. In the past, they'd always closed the offices for Thanksgiving week. Still, he could be tied up with holiday preparations. Maybe.

The sound of my phone ringing had me jumping up and rushing to grab it. Jellie's name lit the screen. Feeling guilty from the crash of disappointment, I took a moment to take a deep breath. She'd pick up on something being wrong if I wasn't careful. Then she'd start throwing more setups at me. More men I didn't want to meet. Knowing her, I'd bet she'd have someone show up for Thanksgiving dinner.

"Good morning," I said as cheerfully as I could. My acting skills weren't the best, but it sounded believable.

"Don't *good morning* me!" she said into the phone excitedly. "Muscular, shirtless, and tattooed, wearing nothing but a towel, and I KNEW NOTHING about this! Spill. Right now!"

Ah. I'd wondered if Thurston would tell Zeke about the other morning. Seemed he finally had.

I pressed the palm of my hand over my heart and winced at the reminder of that morning. All Ransom had said. What

27

we had done. How happy I had been with him. Yet three days later, and I was falling apart.

"And don't give me the *old friend* bullshit you fed Thurst. I know your friends, and you do not have one who fits that description." The accusation in her tone would be funny if I wasn't ready to curl up into a ball and rock in a corner.

"Well, actually, it was the truth. He is from Madison. I tutored him in high school," I replied, wishing we could talk about anything else.

"And … he was randomly in Manhattan, taking a shower in your apartment? Seriously, Noa! I am your best friend! Why did I know nothing about this?! When did you start talking? Did you bump into him when you went back to Madison? How did this happen? And is it going to happen some more?" She almost sounded giddy, except for the small pause she had added when asking about my return to Madison.

Even though Jellie knew my relationship with my mother had been nonexistent, she still treaded lightly when mentioning her.

"We texted on occasion. Then I ran into him again, and we talked a little. It's not a big thing. He's not the kind you have a relationship with." Although, for a moment, I'd allowed myself to think that was what we were doing.

"Yeah, um, okay. This is me. You remember, your bestie? I require details, not a synopsis. That's the right word, isn't it? Synopsis? Oh, never mind. You know what I mean. I want more than that little bit of nothing. I'm not the damn media, looking to do a piece on this. I want to know every second, every little morsel. TALK!"

Sighing, I let my head fall back as I stared up at the ceiling. *God, Jellie. Not today. I do not need this today. I need to mentally*

28

prepare for a weekend with you and your family. Pretending that I'm happy.

"There isn't a big story to tell. He was in town; we met up, had drinks, then came back here. I haven't talked to him since he left."

"UGH! Are you trying to drive me nuts?"

"No, but I have to pack. I would make the story more interesting if there was something to tell." Liar. There was so much to tell. So much I couldn't even tell my best friend.

"We're going to my parents'. All you have to do is toss some sweats into a suitcase and go get on the train."

"I leave for an event on Friday evening. I'm not going home before then."

"Where are you headed to this time?"

"Chicago."

"Signing?"

"Conference. I'm the keynote speaker."

She chuckled. "Your favorite!"

"Yeah, right. You know me. I love getting in front of people and talking." I hated it. Every time I was asked to do it, I wanted to throw up.

"You will be awesome. You always are. I'll look for someone to upload it to YouTube."

I groaned at the reminder that any mistake I made would be forever recorded on the internet.

She laughed. "They love you. Embrace it."

My phone beeped, and I jerked it away from my ear with hope soaring in my chest that it was Ransom. *Unknown* flashed on the screen.

"Uh, I need to get this call. Hold on," I told Jellie, not waiting for her response before clicking Answer.

"Hello?" My voice sounded as uncertain as I was about this.

I normally sent these calls to voicemail, but I was grasping at any chance that Ransom would call me that I was willing to answer anything.

"Do you know where your fiancé is?" a voice that sounded automated, as if it were a computer speaking, asked.

"Um, no," I replied cautiously. What was this? Who was it?

"You should ask."

Frowning, I pulled the phone away and looked down at the screen again, as if it had answers to who this was. "Ask who?" I responded, putting the phone to my ear.

"You know who to ask."

I opened my mouth to argue that when there was a click, and the line was dead.

What in the hell was that?

The word *mob* kept repeating in my brain, and I wondered if that theory was right. Had Arden gotten messed up in something illegal? I could ask Ransom his opinion on what to do … if he'd text me back.

Could I be in danger?

My hand tightened on the phone as I stared at the wall while different what-ifs began to run through my head. A writer's imagination could be a bad thing at times. Like right now. A cold sweat broke out over my body, and I had to gasp for air when I realized I'd been holding my breath.

I was overreacting. That was all. My creative imagination was getting the best of me. This was nothing. Probably some stupid private investigator his parents had hired, trying to scare me into telling him what I knew. Which was nothing.

Clicking back to Jellie, I took a deep breath before speaking. I couldn't tell her about this. If I was in danger, which was unlikely, I didn't want her to also be in danger by association.

"Spam," I said with a sigh before she could ask.

"You need to get that app I told you about! It blocks that shit."

I had the app. It hadn't blocked that caller though.

"I'll do that today," I lied.

nostrils flared as he inhaled
"you go."
ught he might say
ad
l park. I had no response to that. I simply
ps I didn't want

115

FIVE
NOA

The door to the Wattses' two-hundred-twenty-year-old historic Federal home opened, and Melinda Watts squealed with excitement at the sight of Jellie and me. Although it was almost nine at night, she was still dressed as if she were ready to entertain a house full of guests. Complete with heels. I had rarely seen this woman when she wasn't fixed up.

"You're here!" She beamed. "Come in." She stepped back and waved a hand at us. "I have a Crock-Pot of cocoa in the kitchen with all the trimmings."

Jellie let out a pleased sigh as she went inside first, carrying one simple Louis Vuitton duffel bag. "Perfect," she said, then went into her mother's open arms for an embrace.

"I know I saw you last week for lunch, but it's just good to have you home," Melinda told her as she squeezed her tight.

"I know. I brighten up your world," Jellie replied teasingly, then released her mother and moved the rest of the way inside the foyer. "It smells like the holidays."

Melinda turned to me and gave me a welcoming smile, then opened her arms for me. Going in for a hug, I felt a small trickle of emotion and fought back the tears. She was the closest thing I'd ever had to a mother. Something about seeing her made me want to break down about Ransom and tell her everything. I wouldn't though. That was my secret.

"And you too. It wouldn't be the holidays without you here," she told me.

"I wouldn't miss it," I replied.

She patted me back as she held me tightly before releasing me and moving to close the door. "Leave your luggage here. I'll have one of the boys get it up to your rooms," she told us.

"They're here already?" Jellie asked, sounding surprised.

"Of course," Melinda replied. "Tomorrow is Thanksgiving."

"But they live in Portsmouth. They have their own homes. They can just drive over in the morning," Jellie said, then leaned close, lowering her voice. "Is that woman here already too?" she whispered, scrunching her nose.

I knew she was talking about Birch's girlfriend, Ziva or Zeva or Zeda—I couldn't remember. Jellie had not liked her when he brought her to Easter lunch. Honestly, I didn't think any of us had. But then Birch had specific taste in females. He was a photographer and seemed to end up with the models from his photo shoots. I was sure there were nice ones out there, but he always found the arrogant, self-absorbed ones to date.

Melinda shook her head with an amused glint in her eyes. "No. They broke things off in September. She demanded an engagement ring before she left for two months to Italy, and when he said no, she broke up with him."

Jellie blew out a breath. "Thank God," she muttered. "That one was worse than the one before, and Pippie had been bad enough."

33

"Penelope." Birch's deep voice carried over the large, open area, and I turned my gaze up the curved stairway that was the main centerpiece of the entry hall to see Birch descending them with a smirk on his handsome face. "And there was nothing wrong with her."

Jellie let out a hard laugh. "You have a short memory," she told him.

He cocked an eyebrow at her. "Really? Then please enlighten me on what was wrong with Penelope." He emphasized her correct name.

Jellie held up a hand and flipped up one finger. "She had a weird obsession with house plants and talked about them nonstop." She lifted a second finger. "She broke down in a fit of tears when she found out that there was actually turkey in the dressing and not tofu. Wailing about Bambi—who, by the way, is a deer, not a turkey." Her third finger shot up. "She made you go to the store four different times because we didn't have the correct butter or almond milk, and you kept getting some that she swore she could not put in her mouth."

"Okay, I get it. She was a wack," he said, holding up a hand while chuckling.

"Oh, but I didn't get to the best one. The details of her therapist meetings about her fear of belly buttons," Jellie added, then crossed her arms over her chest, looking smug.

I'd forgotten about that one.

"But she was smoking hot and liked kinky shit," Birch replied with a wink.

"OH-kay, that's enough of that. I do not want to hear about any of those details. Please spare me," Melinda announced. "There is hot cocoa in the kitchen to partake in. Birch, will you take the girls' things up to their rooms, please?"

Birch walked over to me and reached down to take my suitcase from me. "Good to see you, Noa," he said. When he moved back with it, he frowned. "Damn, girl, you moving in?"

I shook my head. "No, I'm leaving here on Friday for an event in Chicago," I explained.

He nodded then. "Ah, the famous Juliette Romeo has to make an appearance," he drawled, then gave me a wicked grin. "I read your first book, by the way."

My cheeks heated. Why was Birch reading romance novels?

"And all this time, I had no idea you could read," Jellie chirped.

He rolled his eyes at her, then turned back to me. "I didn't know you had such a naughty streak."

"Leave her alone," Melinda scolded him. "Stop the teasing."

Birch glanced over at his mom. "Oh, I'm not teasing. I'm serious. I couldn't put the shit down."

Melinda held out a hand to me. "Come on, honey. Let's go get you some cocoa, and you can tell me all about life. Jellie said that this Thurston was very interested in you. I want to hear about him and the date."

I swung my gaze to Jellie. Why had she told her that? I didn't like Thurston.

She shrugged apologetically, then turned to look at her mom. "Uh, yeah, about that. Seems she now has a sexy, shirtless, tattooed man sleeping over on occasion, and she's not giving me details. Why don't you get that info out of her instead?"

Birch let out a low whistle. "Tats, huh? Just like the guy in the book. Is that your thing now, Noa?"

No, Birch. It has always been my thing.

Ransom Carver had been my thing since sophomore year. At least I wasn't on the verge of tears anymore. I could give that to the Watts clan. They had successfully distracted me enough to pull myself together. For now.

The massive island in the large, bright kitchen was covered in food. The far-right side was the waffle bar while the other side was meal preparation for dinner. Melinda would be cooking in here most of the day. After the parade, Jellie and I would get dressed and come help her. Mostly chopping vegetables, loading and unloading the dishwasher in the island, and stirring whatever was simmering on the stovetop.

I stifled a yawn and went to the coffee machine, hoping I remembered how this one worked. It had been new last year, and Finton had ended up having to show me how to use it three times before I finally managed to make a successful cappuccino. Frowning, I stared at it before going to get a cup from the cabinet. Jellie was already in the living room, curled up on the sofa with her favorite quilt, waiting on the parade to start. I knew I could ask her to make it, but I didn't want to make her get back up.

A dog barked, and I turned to the tall picture windows lining the dining area across from the kitchen to see Birch with a huge chocolate-colored ball of fluff walking up from the multileveled terrace garden out back. He'd talked about getting another dog last Christmas. His last dog had passed away two years ago from old age. It seemed he'd finally been ready to get another one.

"Any bigger, and it would be a fucking horse," a husky voice said.

I swung my gaze from the man and dog outside to see Finton standing in the kitchen in a pair of green-and-navy plaid pajama pants and a navy T-shirt.

His hair was slightly mussed, and he gave me a sleepy grin. "Mornin', Noa."

Finton was the oldest of the Watts children at thirty-two. He'd been engaged at twenty-seven, but his fiancée had been killed in a skiing accident seven months before their wedding. The tragedy had changed him. He rarely dated. Unlike his brother, he was more serious and focused. Which was probably why he was a successful architect, but he worked too much.

"Good morning," I replied, then glanced back at the dog making its way to the door. "What breed is it?" I asked, not sure I'd ever seen a dog that big.

"Newfoundland," Finton replied, then stretched while yawning. "AKA fucking huge. Mom is making him keep the thing in his bedroom at night. She doesn't want him roaming. She's afraid he'll break shit."

Birch reached the door, and it swung open before his new friend came barreling inside. Its eyes locked on me.

"He doesn't jump—anymore at least. But he likes attention. Best you love on him before you get coffee, or he'll follow you around, begging," Birch said from the open doorway.

Smiling, I set my cup down just as he reached me.

"What's his name?" I asked, bending over to rub his head as he nudged my thigh with his nose.

"Titan," he told me.

"Aren't you just an adorable little bear?" I cooed as he basked in my attention.

"How old is he?" I asked, not looking up from him.

"Eight months," Birch replied.

Finton walked over and picked up my empty cup. "I'll make it. Cappuccino?"

I glanced up at him and nodded. "Yes. Thank you. I'm afraid I don't remember how it works."

He smirked. "I figured."

"TEN MINUTES!" Jellie yelled from the living room. "HURRY UP!"

Titan's head turned toward the noise, and he trotted off in her direction.

"You'd better go stop him before he tries to get on Mom's sofa," Finton said over his shoulder.

"I told him he couldn't do that last night," Birch replied.

Finton made a grunt that sounded like he didn't think that was going to work, but said nothing more.

"Okay, fine. I'll go make sure. But Jellie's squealing would probably scare him off anyway," Birch said. "Make me an espresso while you're at it."

"No," Finton replied.

Birch looked at me, then his brother. "But you're making Noa a cappuccino."

"She can't work the damn machine."

I nodded my head to back that up.

Birch laughed. "Yeah, that's the reason," he said, shaking his head as he headed out of the kitchen after Titan.

What was that supposed to mean? Frowning, I watched him go, then turned to glance back at Finton, who stood silently while the machine finished my cappuccino. The sudden quiet made it awkward—or at least, I felt that way.

"I have to say, I like Titan a lot better than his normal plus-ones during the holidays," I said jokingly, although I did, in fact, much prefer the dog.

"That isn't a high bar. I'd prefer a fucking wild animal to his typical dates," Finton replied as he held out the cup to me.

"Thank you," I told him.

He nodded, but said nothing more before focusing on making himself a cup.

Taking mine, I headed to go join Jellie on the sofa to try and enjoy one of my favorite days of the year while, inside, my heart was aching.

SIX
RANSOM

Closing my bedroom door, I went to the closet and punched in the code for my safe that held my cell phone to see a text from Wayne—the security guard at Noa's apartment complex, who now worked for me. Fuck!

I'd gone down to eat breakfast, and since Bane watched me like a motherfucking hawk, I didn't take this phone with me anywhere that he would be. I was only supposed to have the one phone that Linc had given me. If he knew I'd bought this one, he'd be furious.

Wayne: I have some info on Ms. Raines, sir.

That was all it said. Glancing back at my bedroom door, I double-checked I'd locked it before moving farther away from it and into my en suite and closing that door behind me too. The more barriers between me and anyone who could hear me, the better.

The phone barely rang once.

"Mr. Carver," the older man said over the line.

"What is it?" I barked a little too aggressively.

"Ms. Raines left last night. She had a suitcase with her. Harry was on duty and said that she told him she was going to New Hampshire for the holiday and then on to Chicago from there for a book event. She won't be home until Tuesday."

Dammit! Of course. She always went to Jellie's for the holidays. Portsmouth, New Hampshire. But what event was in Chicago?

"Did she mention the name of the book event?" I asked him as I paced back and forth, feeling like a fucking lion someone had caged.

"No, sir. But Harry said that he asked if it was a signing, and she told him yes, but it was also a conference, and she had to speak at it. Said to cross his fingers that she didn't puke. Something like that."

"Okay. Thanks, Wayne," I told him, then ended the call so that I could go to my web browser and check her website. She had a Signings tab on there that listed her upcoming events.

SpiceCon, November 29–December 1, Chicago, Westin O'Hare.

I clicked the link beside the information. There, on the home page, was Noa's smiling face and a picture of her books. *Keynote Speaker: Juliette Romeo* was written in red calligraphy. The corner of my lips tugged. She would fucking hate speaking in front of people. God, I'd love to be there to watch her. As much as she would hate it, I knew she'd be incredible. Hell, just hearing her voice was enough. I wondered if the attendees knew what lucky bitches they were.

Clicking back to my Contacts, I scrolled down until I found the name I needed. Tapping Ted's name, I put the phone back to my ear. He was a local criminal who did jobs for me that I didn't want the family involved in, and he was the one who had figured out for me that Shakespeare was Juliette Romeo. He was familiar with her after doing the extensive background search on her.

"Ransom," he drawled over the line, sounding like a man looking to get into trouble.

"I need you to find the travel arrangements for Noa Raines this weekend and change them," I said over the line.

"The hot romance writer? Sounds like fun. What'd she do to piss you off?"

"She didn't. I want her flight switched to a private jet. I'll send you the details. You just need to find her travel arrangements and hack into the system to change them. That, and when she arrives in Chicago, I want whatever limo service that was hired to pick her up canceled. I'll handle that mode of transportation."

He cleared his throat. "All right. I'm on it. You know where she's flying out of? JFK?"

"No, try Manchester, New Hampshire and Boston. She's not currently at home."

I waited while I heard the tapping of a keyboard.

"Found it. One Noa Raines. She's got a flight out of Boston on Friday night at seven fifteen, nonstop to O'Hare."

"Good. I'll have what you need from my end in just a few minutes. Stay right there," I told him, then ended the call.

A smirk curled my lips as I imagined her reaction when she got to the airport on Friday and was escorted to the VIP area. Damn, I might have to make a trip, just to watch it from a distance.

SEVEN
NOA

The magical feeling that being at the Wattses' had always brought me for Thanksgiving was absent this year. I'd gone to bed last night, exhausted from constantly acting like I was happy. It wasn't like I hadn't tried to enjoy the holiday. I truly wanted to, but with the silence from Ransom, my heart just grew heavier. I'd thought about something I wanted to tell him at least ten times throughout the day. Things that I knew would amuse him.

I'd wanted to ask him if he'd enjoyed some dressing while I had stuffing with oysters—a Watts family tradition. Or if he'd had sweet potato casserole and pecan pie. The Watts always made roasted root vegetables and pumpkin pie instead. In the past, the food had never mattered. It had been the company. The sense of family and belonging.

But this year ... this year, for the first time ever, I missed the South. The Wednesday before school let out, the school lunchroom would make a traditional Southern Thanksgiving feast. I'd look forward to that meal all month, knowing that the next day, I wouldn't get more than a bologna sandwich and a bag of chips.

I stood, looking at my reflection in the mirror. Melinda had mentioned that my face was thinner and suggested I have seconds more than once yesterday. Then she casually tried to feed me at random times. It was possibly the only thing that was off about me that I couldn't cover up—the sudden weight loss. Birch had picked up on it and started dropping sugar cookies in my lap, telling me to eat up before his mother called an intervention.

Eating when I had no appetite was difficult. I reached up and touched the dark circles under my eyes from lack of sleep. I'd need to cover that up before going down for breakfast. I just had to get through that meal and a few hours of Black Friday shopping in town, and then I'd come back to pack up my things. At least once I left for the airport, I would finally be free to sulk in my misery.

My phone rang, startling me out of my depressing thoughts, and I snatched it up quickly, only to see the name *Unknown* on the screen. I debated answering since the last time I'd had an unknown call, it had been weird and creepy, but I needed to know if it was the same person. If I didn't check, then it would continue to bother me. But then what if it was? I'd had travel, Jellie, and the holiday to keep my mind off the last call. I was leaving today. I wasn't sure I wanted that weighing on me too.

Deciding knowing was best, I hit Answer.

"Hello?" I said cautiously.

"You're in as much danger as he is, you know," the computer-sounding voice said. "Do you know who your friends are?"

I opened my mouth and closed it, not wanting to engage.

"I'll answer that. No, you don't know. You are walking in the Devil's lair and doing it blindly while your fiancé suffers."

Jerking the phone from my ear, I hit End and dropped it onto the counter. *Who was that? What did they want?* My throat felt tight as I breathed hard and fast, trying to tamp down the panic.

I was overreacting. That was just someone messing with me. They were hiding their voice so I wouldn't recognize them. But who would do this? It was sick and twisted. Arden wasn't suffering. He'd run off. He was fine. Probably on a tropical beach, drinking and tanning.

Shaking my head, I turned on the cold water and splashed it on my face, then took a deep breath and let it out slowly. I wasn't answering unknown callers anymore. I wouldn't play this stupid game.

Shopping had somewhat helped get my mind off the weird phone call. Although every time my phone rang, I jumped like it was a bomb about to go off. But now that I was no longer at the Wattses' or with Jellie, my imagination had free rein.

I grabbed the handle on my suitcase, ready to move it to the scale, while the lady behind the check-in counter at the airport looked up my flight information.

"Wait," she said, shaking her head. "You don't check in here."

I frowned. What was she talking about? I started to show her when she picked up a phone and began to call someone. I was getting on this flight. I had confirmation in my email. Jellie was still in New Hampshire, and Birch had dropped me off on his way to visit friends at their house in Nantucket. I didn't want to be stuck in Boston for the night.

"Ms. Noa Raines is here at check-in," the woman said, giving me a polite smile. "Yes. She has two suitcases." The woman glanced over the counter at me. "And a duffel bag."

I'd done my Christmas shopping in Portsmouth, and I had to buy a new suitcase to pack it all in. I was a stress shopper, and I'd overdone it today. As for my duffel, I was going to carry it on. I had originally packed it in my suitcase when I went to the Wattses' for this reason. I'd had luggage delayed before, and I never went without a backup of the necessities in case that happened.

I opened my mouth to tell her that the bag wasn't going to be checked, but she cut me off.

"If you'll wait just a moment, Ms. Raines, our VIP transport will be here to take you and your things to the private lounge to await your departure."

The Sky Lounge? I didn't need a VIP guide to take me there. I could get there on my own just fine. I always did. And I wouldn't call an airline's lounge private. They were normally packed with people.

"Uh, that isn't necessary," I told her, wondering if my publisher had asked for this. And if so, why?

"Yes, it is. For you to get through security to the private hangar, you must be accompanied by one of the FBO staff."

What the heck was FBO? All I knew was TSA.

I just needed to get to my gate and stop in the lounge for a cocktail. She was wasting time.

"I fly a lot, and I've never heard the term *FBO*," I began.

She looked over my shoulder and smiled. "Ah, here he is. George, this is Ms. Raines."

I turned to see a tall man with slick hair and wide shoulders filling out a black suit. This was getting more bizarre by the second.

"Ms. Raines," he said with a head nod, then went to get the handle of the suitcase beside me. "All three of these are yours?" he asked.

"Yes, but could you please explain to me why I'm not checking in here for my flight?" I asked, sounding as frustrated as I felt.

"Those flying by private aircraft don't go through check-in and security here. It's in a different area."

I shook my head. "I'm not flying by private aircraft. I'm flying by this airline," I told him, pointing at the woman at the counter and the sign behind her. "I have my ticket on my app." I started to pull it up when the man grabbed both my suitcase handles.

"Your previous reservation was canceled. You have been booked to fly via private aircraft. If you'll follow me this way," he said, then began to walk away, rolling my suitcases and taking my duffel with him.

My heels clicked against the floor as I hurried to catch up with him.

"I'm sorry. I think there has been a mistake," I called out after him.

He was walking like he was in a freaking race. Or it was his long strides I couldn't keep up with.

"No mistake, Ms. Raines. I have all your details with me."

Okay, so was my publisher doing something new with travel and had forgotten to tell me? Was this some special deal they had gotten?

"No one told me of the change," I explained.

He only nodded his head once again. No other explanation.

This *private plane* thing sounded sketchy.

I was calling Lynette, my agent. She would get to the bottom of this.

47

I wasn't sure who had booked my flights and handled my travel this time. It wasn't always the same person. Typically, it was my publicist's assistant, and that role changed a lot. Hopefully, I wasn't about to fly on some tiny plane that they'd gotten a cheap price on. If so, I'd book my own flight and deal with them later.

"Noa," Lynette said in greeting after one ring.

I continued to almost jog to keep up with the man taking my luggage.

"Something changed with my flight that I hadn't been informed of. They're taking me to some check-in for a private aircraft," I told her. "You know I hate flying, and if this is some tiny plane, I'm not getting on it. I'll book my own flight."

"Huh," she said, sounding as perplexed as I was. "I wasn't told of any new travel arrangements. I'll call and find out what is going on. And don't you dare pay for your flight. If this is a small plane, then they will put you back in first class on the commercial flight, like your contract lists."

I wasn't a diva. Although it sounded like I was being one at the moment. But flying was not my favorite, and I liked having space when traveling. I often wrote while in the air, and first-class seating made that easier.

"Okay," I replied. "I'll try and stall this guy, if I can ever catch up to him."

"I'll be quick," she assured me before ending the call.

Slipping the phone back into my pocket, I tried to talk to the man one more time. "Excuse me," I said. "Could we stop for a moment? I'm waiting on some clarification on this change."

The man didn't slow down. "I heard," he replied. "I can assure you that the aircraft that you are booked on isn't small or cheap."

Scowling at the back of his head, I let out a frustrated groan. It seemed I would have to chase him and my luggage until he was ready to stop. Could this day suck any more?

If he didn't slow down, I was going to be forced to break into a run in my heels. Not something I wanted to attempt. The image of me face down, sprawled out on the floor, flashed in my head, and I pushed it away. I had bigger issues than my possible future embarrassment.

"I'd like to know who changed my reservation because I believe there has been a mistake!" I told him, exasperated.

"There hasn't been," he snapped, not glancing back at me.

Dammit! Could he not stop for a minute and explain this?

As if he read my mind, he suddenly halted and reached into his pocket, where he slid out a slim, flat cell phone in a cherry-red color. Not really something I would have guessed he owned, but I liked it.

"Haze," he said flatly into the phone.

I watched him, catching my breath, and noticed his eyes change, as well as his expression. He visibly paled. Interesting.

"Yes, sir. I'm sorry. Yes." He nodded emphatically. "I understand." The Adam's apple in his throat bobbed, and he quite literally looked ill. Even his broad shoulders and intimidating size seemed to shrink. "Yes, sir." Another hard swallow.

If he lost any more color, he'd match the white walls.

When he slid the phone back into his pocket, his gaze did the briefest sweep of the area around us before they met mine. "I'm sorry, Ms. Raines. I was walking too fast, and I shouldn't have spoken to you so abruptly."

Unexpected, but I liked this much better.

"Yes, thank you, but now that we aren't training for the Boston Marathon, could you please tell me where you got the information that my previous flight was canceled and changed to a private one? I just spoke with my agent, and she knows nothing of this. It's concerning me."

He let go of the handle on one of my suitcases and pulled at his collar, as if it had suddenly become too tight. "Yes, of course," he replied, as if I hadn't already asked this several times and been ignored.

Who had been on that phone call? He'd changed abruptly after hanging up. His boss maybe? But who would that even be, and how would they have known he wasn't being very helpful and was rather rude?

"It seems your original flight was changed to a private jet," he replied, as if that answered my questions.

Although he had used the word *jet* and although I wasn't well informed on aircraft, I had researched the differences between a plane and a jet for a book once. I felt somewhat relieved to hear him call it a jet. That meant it wasn't a tiny twin-prop plane. Which had been my fear at first. I'd flown on one of those from Miami to Key West three years ago with Arden, and I swore I'd never get on another one. The turbulence was horrible, and I'd been in tears by the time we landed.

"But how was it changed? Who changed it?" I asked, not sure if he even had that kind of information.

He shrugged and shook his head, looking apologetic. "I was not given the details, Ms. Raines. I am only told who to go meet to escort to the VIP area for check-in. I'm sorry."

Letting out a heavy sigh, I nodded. "Okay. I guess I will hope for the best."

The tiniest smirk touched his lips, and he quickly changed it to a pleasant smile. "You will be pleased," he replied before reaching down to take the handle of my suitcase again. "I will walk slower," he assured me before turning to continue in the direction we'd been headed.

But I caught it again. His tiny little glimpse of the area around us, as if he was looking for someone and didn't want to be caught doing it. How odd …

Sinking down onto the butter-colored leather seat, I stared around me in awe. What the actual hell? This was … this was a luxury jet. And I was in it alone—well, there were no other passengers at least.

A flight attendant brought me two bottles of red wine. One was a merlot, and the other was … the other was caber-net. Anakota cabernet, to be exact. My favorite. I stared at it, speechless, for several moments while she stood there, wait-ing. My voice cracked when I asked for the cabernet.

She had also left me with a plate of chocolate-covered strawberries. She had informed me the chocolate was glu-ten-free, although I hadn't asked. How had she known about my gluten allergy?

I glanced down at my phone to see if Lynette had called me back to tell me what the hell was going on. Nothing from her. I wasn't complaining about this change, but if the publisher was going to start flying authors around like this, they'd be bankrupt in a month.

I took a sip of wine and sighed as I relaxed. Or tried to. There would be an explanation for all this. I needed to enjoy it and stop trying to figure it out. I'd had a bad week, and this was a nice little escape from my reality at the moment.

Except that I wanted to text Ransom and tell him about it. Ask him if this was how he flew. Take pictures and show him how incredible it was. But I wouldn't do that. He was ignor-ing me or making sure I understood that it had just been sex and now he was done. That stung. No, it hurt like a bitch.

I was tough. I'd survive this.

My gaze dropped to my phone, and I stared at it while I sipped the wine. If he did get around to texting me back, would I be able to act like it was no big deal? Or was this going to destroy what we'd built over the years? The heaviness that hadn't left but had been shoved aside as I dealt with my unexpected change in travel returned full force.

How would I survive this if it was done? All those years of a friendship I had relied on, looked forward to, just over. Finished.

Losing Ransom completely took me to a dark place that perhaps I wasn't strong enough to survive.

EIGHT
RANSOM

Stalking down the concrete stairs into the underground, where we handled things that were unsavory, I glared at the back of Bane's head. I hated the fucking sight of him. Granted, it might not be his fault he was making my life hell, but I needed to get my fury out somewhere. So, he was getting the brunt of it.

I heard a man's pained wail from one of the back caves.

"I thought we were just scaring him into silence," I said. Although the idea of torturing the bastard made my hands itch to release some brutality.

"We are. He's just a fucking bitch. Keeps wailing like he's being tortured." The disgust in Bane's tone was one I recognized.

The PI was going to regret his dramatics if Bane snapped. He could be more ruthless than the rest of us.

But then again, I was walking a real close line to the edge of my sanity. It might be me who snapped. Every second that ticked by, my fucking head taunted me with what Noa was doing, what she was thinking, if she was hurt by my silence, and it was warping my mental stability.

"Shut up," Locke groaned from inside the room, sounding disgusted and annoyed, just before we entered where the PI was being held.

A rope, which hung from the ceiling, was tied around his wrists. There was no blood or bruising on his face. Hell, his feet were firmly on the ground. What the fuck was he wailing about?

"People will know I'm missing!" the man shouted.

Locke rolled his eyes and lit the cigarette that he'd stuck between his lips. "You don't say," he drawled.

"They will! I've left notes. They will know who took me!" he spat out.

That was an issue we'd have to clear up.

"Yet you swore to me you'd told no one anything," Bane drawled.

The PI's face paled as he looked at Bane. He'd suffered some at Bane's hand already. Bane had done a number on him—not physically, but mentally. When Locke had gone to assist Bane in bringing the man from the motel room he was in to here, the man had been in the corner, soaked in his own urine, mumbling about baby giraffes. The scent of his day-old piss clung to the air, making it smell worse down here than it normally did.

"Da-duh-ta-ma." The man began to stammer nonsense as his body trembled.

Locke chuckled. "What psychological shit did you do to this one?" he asked Bane. "He's fucked in the head."

Bane took another step toward the man, and the front of his slacks darkened as he urinated on himself yet again.

"Did you lie to me?" he asked the man.

"Duh-da-duh," he blubbered as his bottom lip began to quiver like a child facing punishment.

"Don't go wack now. Fuck knows you wouldn't shut the hell up before," Locke told him as he inhaled, then let smoke out through his nose. "Seems he documented us. Has a list of our names, families, addresses, and interviewed folks in town stupid enough to talk. He has a list of their names too. We need to go pay some locals a visit." Locke smirked.

"I've got the documentation, his cell phone, his computer, and even the backup drives he stashed in the safe in his motel room," Bane said. "He didn't have proof. Just hearsay." Then he cut his eyes over to Locke. "Gathe, Oz, and Forge are currently paying the chatty locals a visit as we speak."

Bane swung his gaze back to the PI. "But I need to know if there is anything more. Something you're hiding."

More nonsense fell from his lips.

Bane closed the distance between them and grabbed his face, squeezing it with one hand as he jerked him up high enough that his feet dangled above the floor. "Because if you're lying, I'll find out. And I won't just feed you to my hogs. Those people you love, your brother and his wife—you know, the one you keep nudes of to jack off to?" He let out an evil chuckle. "Yeah, I know all about your obsession with your sister-in-law, even if your brother doesn't."

Bane twisted his head to the side hard. If he went just a few more inches, he'd snap it, but he knew that. This angle only caused the man to whimper in pain.

"I don't have a conscience or moral code," Bane told him. "I'll even make sure your sweet, innocent momma pays for your sins," he threatened before shoving him back so that he swung from his arms. "Pull the lever. He doesn't get to touch the fucking ground," Bane told Locke.

Locke reached over and pulled back on the handle that tightened the length of the rope until the man's feet hovered inches from the concrete beneath him.

Bane sneered, "I might just send your brother those photos of his naked wife from your phone for shits and giggles. Let him see what his little brother is up to. Wouldn't that make family gatherings fun?" He paused, then gave the man a bright, amused grin. "That is, if you live to experience another one of those."

"No!" the man bellowed, no longer blubbering like he needed to be committed.

"Well, I'll be damned. He found his words again," Locke said, leaning back to watch with amusement.

Bane cocked an eyebrow at the man. "No?" he repeated. "Do you really think that I care about your wishes at this point?" He pointed at me. "You see this man? The one you trailed? Took photos of, asked questions about?"

The PI said nothing as he stared at me, wide-eyed.

"DO YOU?!" Bane roared this time.

"Y-yes," the man belted out.

Bane nodded, like he was pleased at the response, almost as if he were talking to a small child, explaining something to him.

"He's a fucking asshole when he's unhappy. Impossible to be around," Bane said. "And because of you, he's had something taken from him that has made him a world-class cocksucker." He paused and shook his head. "Not easy to live with."

"I was paid! It was my j-job!" the man blurted out.

Bane tsked. "That's a shame. I suggest you get a new job."

"I w-will duh-duh-ta." He started with the nonsensical words again, and his head twitched.

"Was he this fucked up before, or was this shit all your doing?" Locke asked Bane.

56

Bane gave him a brief glance. "Messed-up childhood from what I dug up. Had inappropriate relations with his aunt, starting when he was twelve."

"I did not!" he cried.

Bane narrowed his eyes at him. "Are you going to lie to me now?"

The man swallowed hard as he stared in horror at Bane.

"Ransom," Bane said.

"Yeah?"

"You have a lot of pent-up anger, don't you? Rage you need to release?"

I nodded my head once.

A sadistic grin curled his lips.

"Why don't you take some of that out on our friend here? He can't seem to remember that I don't like being lied to."

"No, please. I did. I did. She was young though. She came on to me." He began to spill things that I was sure Bane already knew.

"She was ten years older than you, and you fucked her for years. Until you knocked her up when you were nineteen and took her to Mexico to have an abortion that also ended her life. What about that? No one in your family knows why she went to Mexico. Or how she ended up in that low-rent motel room, which was burned to a crisp."

Fucking hell. This man had some dark shit in his past.

He let out a long, high-pitched wail, and his body shook as he began to cry.

I wasn't sure there was anything I could do to this man to cause more agony than Bane's mental attack was doing.

"I didn't know," he blubbered. "I was y-young. Sh-she wasn't s-supposed to d-die."

I shook my head and walked over to the pack of cigarettes Locke had left lying on the bench beside him and

57

tapped one out. Yeah, I was fucking angry. My insides were a damn mess. I wanted to see Noa. Hold her. Fuck her. But beating the hell out of a man in the middle of a complete mental breakdown wasn't going to help me. The dude was already broken.

"Thought you were quitting," Locke said as he held out the lighter to me.

"I was," I said, taking it from him. "That was before."

"If I let you walk out of here alive," Bane said to the man, "will I have to come shut you up permanently, or can you forget all that you learned?"

"I can forget," he sobbed. "I swear it. I can forget it all."

Bane nodded. "Very good. Now, how do you feel about a location change? Somewhere less hectic? Perhaps even tropical? Even a name change would be nice. Don't you think?"

The door to my office opened, and my head snapped up. An angry snarl curled my tongue, as I was ready to lash out at whoever was interrupting me. I'd had little sleep in the past two weeks, and my mood had gone from bad to murderous. Having my every fucking move monitored was making it worse.

Oz Savelle stepped into the room and closed the heavy oak door behind him. The expression on his face told me whatever this was about, it wasn't going to help my mood.

"What?" I asked, wanting him to just tell me and leave.

He held up both hands. "I don't want to be here either," he replied defensively. "But Bane said if you snapped at him one more time, he was going to plant his fist in your face. So, here I am."

Saying nothing, I waited. Linc had sent shit through Bane for the past fourteen days. Orders, warnings, bullshit. He had been stalking me. And until now, I hadn't known just how efficient he was at it.

Oz took a drink from his bottle of water, then sighed. "You know this will all blow over eventually. The PI has been taken care of. He might never speak again after the shit we put him through."

"What are you here to tell me?" I asked, wanting him to just say it and leave. I didn't need consoling.

"Bane said to tell you that you were sloppy."

My eyes narrowed as I stared at him, trying to decide what it was Bane knew.

Oz shrugged. "He didn't tell me anything more. Whatever he knows, he's not saying. But whatever you did, he's not happy about it, and he's protecting you with his silence."

I hadn't been sloppy. I'd been thorough. But there was no point demanding more from Oz since he was just the messenger.

"I don't know what he's talking about," I grumbled, looking back down at the paperwork on my desk.

"Yeah"—Oz chuckled—"you do."

I lifted my eyes back to him as he turned and walked out of the door.

What had I been sloppy with? Did Bane know I'd been tracking Noa? Taking care of things for her? Making sure she had everything she needed?

She'd fucking cried last night before she fell asleep. I'd had to watch it and suffer through it, not being able to do shit about it. There were times I hated the fucking cameras I'd snuck back into her apartment to install while she was in New Hampshire. But then seeing her every day was the only thing keeping me sane.

I hadn't been to her apartment since she had returned from Chicago. I'd been there to make sure she arrived home safely.

Watched her sleep, then left. Was that what Linc knew? And if so, why was he just now saying something? It had almost been a week since then.

So, what was it he had sent Bane in here to warn me about? I'd not gone back to see her, although she was ripping my chest open with her tears every night. He had nothing to bitch about. If he knew about the private plane I had hired for her travel or the one I'd used to go to put the cameras in her apartment or for the night she returned home, I would have heard something about it by now.

Fuck that, if he'd known, he'd have been waiting on me at the airstrip. I'd left no traces of my trip. He couldn't know I'd been there.

Unable to focus on the orders in front of me, I jerked open my desk drawer and pulled out the phone they didn't know I had. Clicking it open, I went to the cameras in Noa's apartment and checked each one until I found her in front of her desk, chewing on the end of a straw while glaring at her computer screen.

She'd done more of that than actual writing since returning from Chicago. She also muttered a lot. The words I could hear often had my name in them. My silence was hurting her, and I fucking hated it. Every time I watched her and knew the sad look in her eyes was because of me, I wanted to destroy everything in my path. It was a miracle I hadn't broken a fucking tooth with all the grinding I'd been doing, trying to keep it together and not completely snap.

Watching her get on the private jet I'd gotten for her trip to Chicago and not being able to follow her onboard had been brutal. I was limited to making sure she had all she could want or need for her flight. The cocksucker I'd chosen from the FBO employees almost lost a few fingers, possibly his goddamn tongue, for his treatment of her. But when I called him to correct his rude behavior, he was excellent, so I hadn't sliced off one of his digits with my blade.

She took the straw from her teeth and tossed it across the room, then let out an exasperated growl before standing up. Planting her hands on her hips, she let her head fall back. "UGH! This is all your fault, Ransom Carver! You heartless son of a bitch."

My lips quirked. "Call me names if it helps, Shakespeare. But you'll forgive me. I swear it."

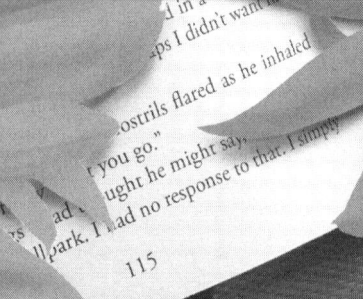

NINE
NOA

Twenty Days Since Ransom Left …

I hadn't left my apartment in thirteen days. Almost two weeks. It was just sad. If I had more than twenty thousand words written on my manuscript, I wouldn't feel like such a loser about it. My not leaving would have had a purpose. But seeing as I had barely written any words, cried more than I wanted to admit, and avoided most of Jellie's calls, it was, in fact, depressing. As if I needed more cause to be depressed. Ransom had sunk me to the lowest of my lows in that area of my life.

Christmas in New York was always a magical time that I savored every moment of. My tree would go up the weekend after Thanksgiving, and I'd begin wrapping gifts, making apple cider, and playing holiday music over the sound system. This year, I'd done nothing. I avoided even looking out my window at the cheerful lights and festive decorations lining the streets.

It was eleven days until Christmas, and the suitcase I'd bought in Portsmouth was still packed with the gifts I'd bought, sitting in the corner of my bedroom. I'd yet to even open it. Tomorrow was the first day of Hannukah, and most of the employees at the publishing house would be on their holiday vacation to bring in the season. I should have taken the gifts I'd bought for my editor, marketing director, and former boss. I didn't have it in me to even pretend to be happy.

After getting out of bed this morning, I'd taken a shower, forced myself to put on clothing appropriate for leaving the apartment, and made plans. Well, okay, my plans were to go to my favorite local bookstore, treat myself to a gluten-free Christmas sugar cookie at a bakery nearby, and pick up some much-needed groceries instead of having them delivered. Living in seclusion wasn't good for my mental health. I also needed a distraction from my thoughts about Ransom. Maybe the smell and feel of the holidays on the busy streets would do that for me. Staying inside alone sure hadn't helped. I was only sinking deeper into my dark hole.

The fact that I'd drunk an entire bottle of wine last night, then texted Ransom was my breaking point. When I opened my eyes this morning, I checked my phone. Of course, I had gotten no response. It was humiliating in the light of day. Sober me was never going to drink again. My pathetic *I miss you* text was taunting me. If only I could erase it. Like the others I'd sent, my drunken one had also been left unread. I guessed I should be thankful for that. I didn't want him to see it. But … had he blocked me? Was he not seeing the texts from me at all? Would he do that?

The ache in my chest sank to my stomach and caused it to knot up painfully. I hated this feeling. I did miss him. At least ten times a day, I'd think of something I wanted to tell him, but when I reached for my phone, I'd remember he wasn't talking to me.

I had been ghosted.

I'd become one of those.

The females that Ransom fucked, then ditched.

And as mind-blowing and earth-shattering as sex had been with him, I'd go back and change it if it meant I'd get to keep him in my life. I could live without the sex. I didn't want to live without Ransom. Even if it was just texting. He was a necessity in my life.

But I'd been weak. I thought that I was different. I was foolish enough to believe Ransom Carver needed me in his life too. How freaking naive I'd been. He didn't need any one female. All it would take for him to replace me was one snap of his fingers, and they'd come running. He probably had my replacement already. Someone who was thrilled to receive his texts. Did he send her random facts about whiskey? Did she respond with pointless facts she'd researched that day? Highly doubtful. Didn't he miss our little quirky back-and-forths? Was I truly that forgettable?

If I hadn't already been in a dark place, I had just gotten myself in a deep, endless pit now.

Sighing, I grabbed my purse, determined to find some peace today. Or just a break from the pain. Anything to distract me. Ease up the constant sorrow that his absence caused.

Maybe then I could talk to Jellie. She was going to show up at my door soon if I didn't. I'd avoided her because she knew me too well. If she heard my voice, she'd know I wasn't okay. Then she'd want details, and she wouldn't give up until I spilled everything.

Some things were just too painfully humiliating to share. Even with her.

How I was going to do Christmas at the Wattses' this year, I didn't know. I'd passed the point of pretending I was okay. They'd all see it—and not just because I'd lost even more weight from my lack of appetite. My eyes even looked empty when I stared at myself in the mirror. This year, I might have to be sick for Christmas. Perhaps tell them that I had tested positive for COVID and hide away, wrapped in my misery, here in this apartment.

The smell of the city wasn't always pleasant, but the bakery two doors down filled the air with the scent of holiday cheer. I took a moment to enjoy it before turning in the opposite direction and heading toward the bookstore I frequented. This had once been an every Sunday outing for me. But my Sundays had become workdays, as did every day as of late. Or *sit and stare at the screen* days was more like it.

"Noa!"

I paused and turned around at the sound of my name before I registered whose voice it was.

Thurston was walking in my direction with a to-go cup of coffee in one hand and a smile on his face. I hadn't wanted to see anyone I'd have to actually converse with. In a city with over one-point-six million people, crammed into twenty-two-point-sixty-six square miles, it didn't happen often.

Lucky me.

It took great effort not to roll my eyes as he approached me. I was in a bad mood. The worst of my life, but it wasn't his fault. He'd done nothing wrong.

"Good morning." I managed a smile.

"Yeah, it is now," he replied, and then his brows drew together. "I wasn't sure if I'd see you again. The unanswered texts and refusal to answer my calls made it clear you were pissed at me. I wanted to apologize for that. The thing in your apartment ... I shouldn't have shown up unannounced. I'm sorry."

I didn't want a reminder of that day. Ransom came with the memory. Other than Ransom being rude to Thurston and ordering me around, I'd been happy then. Living in a brief bubble of joy that had burst all too soon.

Wait … what texts and calls? He hadn't contacted me. The tiniest shred of hope started to spark inside my chest.

"I, uh, didn't get any texts or calls from you," I said.

Was something wrong with my phone? Had Ransom been trying to text me or call me? Was that it?!

But Jellie's calls and texts had come through. So had my editor's. Maybe it was just certain numbers. Or possibly bad service. I was grasping here, and I knew it.

"I called at least three times and texted more. Jellie said to just give you some time. You were busy with work and not talking to her much either."

I pulled out my phone to double-check. It was stupid, but if there was the slightest chance that Ransom had been having the same problem, I needed to know. He could think I was the one ghosting him. Well, except for the four texts I had sent that he hadn't read.

I found Ransom's name first and checked to see my texts still sitting there, ignored. The little bubble was slowly deflating. I went to search Thurston's name, but it wasn't in my Contacts. Nor were there any texts from unnamed numbers.

"I've not gotten anything from you," I told him as I turned my screen off and slid my phone back into my pocket.

He opened his phone, then handed it to me. "I sent them," he said. I looked down at the texts to my name and number. "I can show you the calls too. If you'd like."

I shook my head. "No. I believe you. I just … something must be wrong with my phone service."

"What about that brunch? Or did you have another engagement?"

Brunch. With him.

I wanted to go back to my apartment, curl up on my bed, and wallow. Forgo the attempt at holiday cheer. It hadn't been working anyway.

But I had to do something about my state of mind. Another drunken night alone, texting a man who was ignoring me, would not happen again.

I nodded. "That would be nice."

Getting out and living was a step I needed to take. One that would lead to moving on with my life. At least I hoped it would. One day.

He beamed at me. "Excellent. I was eighty percent sure you were going to turn me down."

My laugh was forced and fake, but he didn't seem to notice.

"I haven't eaten yet. I was going to just pick up something after I stopped by the bookstore," I told him. I had no appetite, but I needed to eat.

"Perfect timing. Looks like fate took over for me," he replied with a flirty grin.

I didn't try to smile back, but nodded my head once. I didn't much care for fate. It had a way of screwing me over. Like right now.

Taking a bite of the only gluten-free option available at the place Thurston had brought me to, I tried to act like I cared about his week at work. At least he liked to talk about himself. I wasn't required to say much or answer any questions. Remembering to nod and appear as if I were listening was a challenge though. I was getting weary from listening alone.

We'd not even been here thirty minutes, and I was bored to tears. The gluten-free French toast was good at least.

Although I wasn't going to be able to eat much of it. My stomach had shrunk from my lack of eating the past two weeks. As had the rest of me. I'd had to take off my jeans and put on a sundress because they were too big.

"That is, if you are free that weekend? Jellie mentioned that you normally spent Christmas with her family in New Hampshire, but I wasn't sure how long you stayed after the actual day," I heard him say and realized I had no idea what he was talking about. I'd zoned out. He was watching me with anticipation, but I didn't know what I was supposed to be saying.

Had he invited me somewhere? If so, I was busy. Very busy, sitting in my apartment alone. Writing—or trying to write. There was no way I was going anywhere with him. This was punishment enough. I wasn't mentally ready to attempt dating of any kind.

"I, uh—"

The sound of an alarm went off, startling me and jerking Thurston's steady gaze off me to look toward the kitchen, where it seemed to be coming from. Talk about saved by the bell.

"Fire!" a man yelled as he came barreling out from the kitchen entrance. "Everyone, out!"

Dropping my fork, I grabbed my purse and quickly jumped up, not waiting to see if Thurston was coming. Other customers were hurrying for the exit, and more alarms joined the first one, making it impossible to hear anything else. I made my way behind the first rush of those leaving before glancing back to see Thurston carrying his breakfast sandwich in one hand and his cup of coffee in the other. Apparently, he didn't want to leave his food behind. There were more shouts to move quickly and away from the building as we were pushed into the others on our way out.

"Come this way," Thurston shouted behind me when we were finally outside, then turned right.

I followed him down the street a short way before the fire department sirens began to blare.

I should have stayed in today.

"My apartment building is four blocks this way and then a right turn and two more blocks," he told me when we were far enough away that he didn't need to shout. "You could come up for a cup of tea if you want. I just got a tree yesterday, and I was going to decorate it today. I'd love the help."

Nope. That was absolutely not happening. I wanted nothing to do with decorating his tree or seeing his apartment. The universe had handed me an out, and I was taking it.

"Thanks, but I've got a bit of a headache after that, and I need to get to work. I'm very behind on my manuscript."

His flash of disappointment was brief before he was smiling again. "Well, we can just plan on finishing our date another time," he replied.

No, we can't.

"Go get your phone checked out and give me a call or text when you have some free time."

"Okay," I said, knowing that day would never come. "Should we go back and pay?" I asked, realizing we'd not received our check before we were evacuated.

He shook his head. "I'll call and handle it later. They're busy at the moment."

Thankfully, I would need to turn left at the next intersection, and we could part ways. My bookstore trip wasn't going to happen today. I didn't want to chance him deciding to come along. Staying inside alone might have been better for my mental health after all.

TEN

RANSOM

Her apartment was dark and silent. I checked each camera while drinking straight from a bottle of our special label whiskey. If I didn't drink myself to sleep, I wasn't going to get any. Today had been shit, and it had nothing to do with the shipment that had gotten destroyed in a trucker accident or the wrong labels that had been ordered. Nope. All that I could handle. I'd done it before.

For the first time in my life, I was drinking over a woman. An ironic chuckle passed my lips, and I felt the buzz from the alcohol seeping through me. Oh, how the mighty had fallen.

I couldn't even get annoyed with my brother being up his girl's ass. Fuck, I wished Noa were in my bed. That I had the ability to see her all I wanted. Another first for me. I was jealous of Than. He was so damn high on life right now that I could hardly stand to be around him. I'd been ready to pick him up and throw him through the window in my office today to shut him up. He'd been going on and on about my coming over to see their Christmas decorations.

He was loving every moment of the holidays while I hated opening my eyes every morning, knowing it would be another day that I had to go without contacting Noa. One more day that she'd think I had tossed her aside. Today, I'd almost snapped. Walked out of this house, got on a plane, and said fuck it to all of them. Let Blaise hunt me down and put a bullet in my head. But I would thankfully live to see another day. I'd thought it through and handled things when I realized she'd gone to motherfucking brunch with that douchebag.

Having another man disappear would only make my situation worse. So, I was smart. Even if, for a brief second, slicing the Ken Doll up into small pieces had crossed my mind when the girl who had answered the phone at the restaurant, where the tracker said Noa was at, described the jackass at the table with her.

I might not be the best at mind games like Bane was, but I could manipulate people. Use their weaknesses and needs against them. It hadn't been hard to get what I wanted from the restaurant owner when I called him. Like most people, money was the bargaining chip I needed, and it worked beautifully. He did exactly as I'd instructed him to. I'd not been sure he would at first. Asking someone to set fire to their own business wasn't normal, but it was the best solution. The other being me disobeying orders and hauling my ass to Manhattan to kill a man.

Yep. That was where I was. Ready to murder a guy for getting too close to what was mine.

"What's got you so enthralled? Porn?"

I glanced up at the sound of Bane's voice, expecting to see him with Hawkins in his arms. Instead, he was alone with a glass of water.

"Why are you up?" I asked.

He shrugged. "Got thirsty. And although Hawks has started sleeping again all night, I'm now on some fucked-up schedule where I wake up anyway."

I grunted, not really interested and wanting him to leave me to my live video feed of Noa sleeping and my whiskey. He continued into the room, and I clicked off the screen, not wanting him to see what I had been watching. Let him think it was porn. That was better than him knowing the truth.

"It's not porn then," he drawled with a smirk and sank down on the leather chair across from me. With a tilt of his head in the direction of my phone, he added, "You wouldn't have shut that down because I walked in."

Shut up, Bane. Go away. Let me drink and stalk my girl in private.

My girl.

Was she? Yeah, she fucking was. She had been for years. I'd just not realized it.

"Your girl?" he asked, his brows drawing together.

Shit. I'd said that out loud. Maybe I was more than buzzed.

"Go to bed," I mumbled, then took another drink from the bottle.

"Oh, hell no. Not after that comment. Who are you calling your girl? And please, for Christ's sake, tell me it's not the writer. I'm not up for trying to keep your ass alive if Blaise finds out you're still in contact with her."

I stared at him as I took a long pull. Blaise could suck my dick, along with Linc. Both of them had their women. They'd not been ordered to stay away from them. Assholes.

"I'm here. I've not talked to her in twenty days, and she went on a motherfucking date this morning. Had brunch with some asswipe," I snarled.

Bane winced. "I'd ask how you know she went on a date, but I'm guessing you've still got trackers on her," he said, and then his eyes went to my phone, which I still clutched tightly in my hand. "Ah fuck. Are you watching her? You've got video cameras on her? Tell me you're not pulling Oz's fucked-up shit."

I said nothing. Fact was, my stalking might be worse than Oz's had been. He'd never put a camera in Winslet's bedroom. And he'd not paid a man to set a fire in the kitchen of his restaurant so that it had to be evacuated to end a date that she was on. I bit back a grin. That had been rather brilliant of me.

"What?" Bane asked, his eyes widening. "Did you fucking say what I think you did?"

Dammit, I was still talking out loud.

I shrugged. Whatever. It wasn't like he was a saint. He'd sliced Halo's throat before he fell in love with her. He was the damn psycho. Not me. I was just taking care of what was mine.

"Best way to clear a place out is a little fire," I replied, then chuckled before taking another drink.

Bane shook his head. "Jesus, you're nuts, and I thought you were the sane one."

"Desperate times and all," I replied as if that excused my actions.

"How much did you pay him?"

I set the bottle between my legs and sighed. "Six months' rent. Immediate wire into his account the second I had live footage from his phone of the restaurant being evacuated and Noa rushing out the door. He was already behind two months on his lease of the place, so he was desperate. That was just fucking luck."

Bane leaned back in his chair and blew out a breath. "Damn."

"It was better than killing her date," I mused. Which I still might do. If he didn't stay the fuck away from her.

"Or selling him to the cartel," Bane added with a shake of his head, then took another drink of water. "You've got some twisted shit in your head. We need to be using it for more than your obsession with this woman."

"Not an obsession," I bit out through clenched teeth, annoyed.

"Then label it," he shot back at me.

Label it? Was there a label for it? I sat there, staring straight ahead, as I dissected the way I felt. How I reacted to her.

Finally, I looked back at Bane. "A necessity."

Bane blew out a breath and stood back up. "Ah. So, you're in love."

No, the fuck I was not. This wasn't about love. I required Noa in my life. She was indispensable. There was no one else that centered me or made me feel … whole. Balanced things for me. Cleared the shit from my head. She gave me peace.

"And that, my friend, is what love is," Bane drawled with amusement. "Welcome to the club."

I watched him as he walked toward the door, headed back to bed with his wife. Apparently, I'd had so much to drink that I was speaking all my thoughts without realizing it.

"I'm not in love," I called out after him. "That's a fucking dumb emotion. It makes you weak. Messes up your head. Controls you."

Bane stopped and turned back around. He raised one of his eyebrows as he stared back at me. "And you sitting in here, watching her sleep on the hidden cameras you placed in her apartment, isn't you being controlled? Your head was clear today when you decided to pay a man to set a fire in his place of business? Or when you handed a man over to the cartel without going through the line of authority?"

I said nothing.

"Right. That's what I thought," he finally said.

When he walked away this time, I let him go. Bastard had said shit I didn't need to hear.

Swiping my finger over my phone screen to open up the camera I'd been watching before he interrupted me, I sighed heavily. Just the sight of her eased me. Not completely because I wanted to talk to her. Reassure her. Explain why I had gone silent. But it did help me breathe.

Ah fuck.

Bane might be right.

Dammit all to hell!

ELEVEN
NOA

Twenty-Eight Days Since Ransom Left ...

While my manuscript had needed me to stay inside tonight and continue to work on it, my sanity required I get the hell out of the apartment. Not that I was counting ... okay, I was counting ... but it had been four weeks of silence from Ransom. It was time to face the fact that we were over.

The bouquet of sunflowers, arrangement of chocolate-covered caramels, and all three volumes of the first printing of *Pride and Prejudice* that had been delivered over the past week were maddening and confusing. Thurston hadn't called or texted, so I assumed he'd gotten the hint, and I had a hard time believing he'd sent these specific gifts. Each delivery had been an exact replica of items given to the heroine in my first two books. The *Pride and Prejudice* set had sent me reeling. The price on those was a quarter of a million dollars. I'd looked it up online when I wrote the gift into my story.

The only person I knew who could spend that kind of money would be Ransom, but he was ghosting me, so that made no sense. It would also mean he'd read all of my pub-lished books thus far since the *Pride and Prejudice* set was the wedding gift the hero gave the heroine in the last book. My ideal Ransom I'd created in my head. The real Ransom wanted to shut me out of his life. He had fucked me and was moving on. It was what he did. He didn't send elaborate gifts, and he didn't read romance novels. As far as I knew, he'd just read the first one.

I stared at the books I'd put in a firesafe glass display case and placed on my bookshelf. They baffled me the most. Even if someone had been lucky enough to inherit these, why would they just give them away? And to me?

Thoughts of Arden, which were rare, flickered through my head, and I wondered if it was possible. He had read all my books. He'd edited them. He knew my characters as well as I did. Would he have sent them? His way of apologizing? The wedding gift from my novel could hold some significance. But where would he have gotten that much money to buy something so expensive? This wasn't a typical Christmas gift. It was on another level.

Grabbing my purse, I took a deep breath and went to the door. I normally didn't go out in the evenings by myself, but this was Manhattan, and it never slept. Especially this close to Christmas. Stores were staying open later, and people were rushing to shop after getting off work. It would be busy and full of tourist.

I'd walk until I saw something that I thought I could actu-ally eat more than one bite of. I needed to eat today. Going all day without food wasn't good for me, but it was becoming the norm.

I also needed to pick up some more laundry detergent, and if Ulta was still open, I was almost out of my sham-poo. With a plan before me, I headed down the elevator and exchanged good evenings with Wayne, who had been work-ing a lot more shifts these days. I saw him more than any of the other security doormen.

When I stepped outside onto the always-busy street, the sound of horns blaring was comforting. I'd once hated it. They always startled me, but over time, I'd come to think of them as normal. Part of the city. Inside the apartment, the noise was muffled, and I often didn't notice it. Glancing up and down the street filled with elaborate holiday window displays, I gave myself a small pep talk about finding some joy in this. This was my favorite time of year, and I had been missing it, locked away in my apartment.

I turned left and started down the street toward the busier section, where there would be more food options. However, I could take the side road up ahead and make a little detour. If the rare bookstore two streets over was still open, I could stop inside and inquire about the difficulty to find the *Pride and Prejudice* first-edition set and possibly show them the photos I'd taken of them to get their opinion. My need to know who had sent the books centered around my small strands of hope that Ransom wasn't truly gone from my life. That he felt something. Maybe he had shut me out because of that? Because he was scared of feeling something more than friendship?

I knew the more I spent dwelling on that and clinging to it, the harder reality was going to hit me when the weeks continued to pass with no word from him.

There was also the fact that when I'd had yet another bot-tle of wine last week while wallowing in my heartache, I had called him. Foolish, but I did it. And the number had been disconnected. That should be a big, bright neon sign right there, telling me that Ransom was gone. He was closing all connection with me.

He had not sent me gifts that were in my stories. Especially not gifts that could buy someone a decent-sized home in Madison. Here, it would be a nice downpayment. And the colorful, expensive wrapping paper that they'd been in wasn't very Ransom-like either.

I paused at the street I was going to cross and glanced down to my right. It was only eight. The bookstore might possibly still be open. It was three days to Christmas, and people were out, shopping for those last-minute gifts. There was a good chance it would be. I'd google it to check and see, but I couldn't remember the name of it. I had passed it dozens of times, but the rare books in the windows always caught my eyes. The street was quieter, but it wasn't a long one. I was also a fast walker. If I got nervous, I'd run.

Slipping my hand into my purse to get out my small can of pepper spray, I clenched it tightly and headed toward the bookstore. The more I thought about who had sent the books, the more I believed it was Arden. He would assume I'd know it was him and not think he had to put a card with it. That made the most sense.

It also was such a devastating thing to admit that it made my chest tighten and my eyes water. I didn't want it to be Arden. I didn't want it to be Thurston—although I was ninety-five percent sure it was not. I wanted it to be Ransom.

I missed him. It wasn't getting easier as the days passed. The pain was getting more intense. Wasn't time supposed to heal? I needed it to freaking hurry the hell up.

A door opened a few feet ahead of me, and a man stepped out, wearing a pair of jeans and a black hoodie. Two cars had driven by since I'd started down this street, but other than a couple on the other side of the road, walking in the opposite direction, I hadn't passed anyone else. The lack of stores made this street empty compared to the one I'd been on before.

The man paused and turned to look at me. The turn-and-flee reaction was typical for someone who watched crime television the way I did. If there was more lighting, it wouldn't feel as if I were walking into danger. This was mostly residential. People were in their apartments, so they'd see if something went on down here …

But this was New York City. Did people even pay attention to what was happening on the streets? Murders were committed on these streets all the time.

STOP, NOA! It is just a man wearing a black hoodie with … possibly a tattoo on his face. Or is that a birthmark? Does it matter? No. Unless I need to ID him later. That would make it easier. But to ID him would mean I'd survived whatever he did to me.

Good Lord, listen to my thoughts. He isn't going to do anything to me.

I kept walking, although my grip on the pepper spray was tighter, and my finger moved to the trigger. I forced a tight smile and looked away from him, although he was still watching me and kept walking at the same pace. It was likely he could run faster than me.

Don't tempt the bear. Just walk casually.

"Pretty lady," he called out just as I reached where he stood. "I have purses. Designer."

I just bet he did. *Join thousands of others on these streets.* "No thank you," I replied and kept going.

"Louis Vuitton. Authentic. You want to see? Yes! Prada," he continued, and his footsteps fell into step behind me.

Dammit. I should have stayed on the shopping district street.

"No thanks," I said as my steps quickened.

"Gucci! You like? Luggage too. Just inside. Come see. I will give you good price."

Come inside and never be seen again? Not happening, buddy. Go away.

"No thank you," I repeated more firmly.

His footsteps sounded as if he was getting closer to me and doing it rapidly. Panic was starting to bloom in my chest as the reality that I might possibly be in danger sank in. I'd not been cautious. I'd come out alone and taken off down a road I never traveled by myself on foot. All because of those damn books.

Just as I lifted my hand, ready to aim the can at his face and spray him, his hand wrapped around the upper part of my arm and jerked it hard enough that the pepper spray fell from my grasp and landed at my feet.

A scream welled up in my throat as he pulled me backward and spun me around to face him. I scrambled to keep from losing my balance. I was not going to become one of the missing people who ended up on the news. The fight to free myself overrode my fear, and I kicked at him while struggling to free my arm.

I was just about to claw at his face when a shadow fell over him. My eyes shot up to see a larger man step out of the darkened street and into the streetlight. He, too, was wearing a hoodie.

Shit! Were there two of them? I was going to be abducted. Shipped off and never seen again. I didn't even have my freaking pepper spray!

"What the—" The man holding me paled and stilled. His eyes went wide.

Confused, I looked at him, then shot my gaze back up to the figure, whose face was still hidden from me. He was now towering over the man whose grip on my arm was cutting off blood circulation.

"Unless you want this blade to go directly into your spinal cord, you'll let go of her."

The deep voice sent a rush through me. Recognition, emotion, and relief hit me all at once, and I let out a sob. The man's hand was gone instantly, and he held both his hands up.

"I was just going to give her a good deal on designer p-pur-rses," he stammered.

"She said no thanks," Ransom replied, and his voice made me shiver.

"I will leave her alone."

"Yeah, you will," he agreed before the man was slung back toward the door he'd exited.

He stumbled and caught himself before falling backward.

The man glared at Ransom now that he no longer had Ransom's blade pressed to his back. An evil sneer slid over my would-be abductor's face, and he pulled a knife of his own from the pocket of his hoodie and lunged toward Ransom.

Where was my pepper spray, dammit?! I dropped my gaze to the ground, looking for my lost can. Ransom had saved me, and I wasn't about to let this thug hurt him.

"Bad idea," Ransom snarled.

I snapped my gaze back to see what was happening just as the other man cried out in pain, his body jerking in an unnatural way before he bent at the waist.

"That was your lung. Might want to get that checked out before you die," Ransom said.

Die? What?

I looked at Ransom for some kind of reassurance that no one was dying, but he stood there, his jaw clenched, glaring at the man with an expression that caused me to take a step back. It was unnerving, savage, hellish even.

Ransom's gaze dropped to the ground, and then he bent down to get something. I took another step back, needing space. From all of this.

Ransom had just stabbed a man. Possibly killed him. I reluctantly flickered my gaze back to the other man. Even in the darkness, the lack of color in his face was apparent. He was pale. Unnaturally so. There was blood trickling from the corner of his mouth now. He didn't reach up to wipe it away or spit. Instead, he rasped in a breath with such difficulty that his body slumped over even further.

"You need a Taser. This shit is worthless," his deep, husky voice said as he straightened, holding the lost can of pepper spray.

"You-you're here," I choked out. Not, *You just stabbed a man*, or, *I think he is dying*. No, I didn't say either of those things. My first words were *you're here*. That didn't say a lot for my moral code.

He studied the can in his hand as the man behind him continued to make unnatural noises—I wasn't sure if they were from pain or the fight to breathe. Ransom ignored him completely. We stood there for a few moments, saying nothing. The world around us felt as if it had gone quiet.

"No, I'm not," he finally said, lifting his eyes back to mine. What did that mean?

"Go back to your apartment. I'll clean this up."

What? No.

I shook my head. I was not leaving him. I hadn't seen him or spoken to him in a month. Now, he was suddenly here, playing vigilante.

"I haven't—you've not—"

"Shakespeare. Go. I need to handle this."

His tone was firm, but the way he'd said Shakespeare sent warmth coursing through me. Something I shouldn't be feeling at this moment. I should be ashamed of being able to feel any joy while there was a death happening feet away from me.

"But—but you've been gone." The fear that he'd vanish again kept my feet firmly planted. I wasn't letting him disappear out of my life again.

He nodded his head. "Yeah."

The man began to make gurgling sounds that snapped me out of my own problems and back to the most pressing issue.

Ransom cut his eyes toward him. "Seems I got more than his lung," he muttered, then turned back to me, "Go," he repeated.

If someone found us and Ransom was caught with the bloody knife, he'd be arrested. I had to let him do whatever it was he did in situations like this. The idea that he'd go to prison over his saving me was enough to make me move. I wouldn't lose him again.

"You need to get out of here," I told him, wanting him to come with me.

"I got this, Shakespeare. I know what to do. But you need to go."

He wasn't going to just leave the man here like this. I knew that. I was being selfish, even asking him to. The man began to shuffle and fall to the side.

Oh God. Was he dying? Was I about to witness my first death?

"Shakespeare, go," he urged.

As much as leaving him was difficult, I had to believe once he had this handled, he'd come to me. We would talk. He hadn't just been on this street for an evening stroll. He was here for me. He'd been following me. I had questions, but they could wait.

Turning, I began to walk back the way I had come from. Ransom was back in my life. He had returned.

While my body was slowly feeling the relief and joy, there was also guilt invading my happiness. Glancing back over my shoulder, I saw Ransom moving over to the man.

Was he going to get him help? Did the Mafia do that kind of thing?

It had just been one stab wound. It wasn't like he'd shot him. He just needed a doctor ... or an emergency surgery.

It was fine. Ransom knew what to do. He'd handle it, and then he'd come to me. And my world would be right again.

TWELVE
RANSOM

"WHAT the FUCK, Ransom?" Bane shouted as he slammed into my office without knocking.

I'd been expecting him after the text I sent him from my secret phone. And I'd also been anticipating this reaction. He was right, but he'd have done the same damn thing.

"Can we skip the drama?" I asked, leaning back in my chair and crossing my arms over my chest.

"The drama?" he asked incredulously. "You disobeyed a direct order and stabbed a man in the process. You left a trail by killing someone. That's not fucking drama!"

"Eh, I didn't leave a trail. I cleaned up my mess," I replied.

Bane let out an unamused laugh. "You've gone insane. It's two days until Christmas. I want to enjoy my holiday, not deal with your bullshit!"

"Could you keep your voice down?" I asked him, not wanting Than to hear any of this.

Bane stood there, glaring at me like he wanted to toss me through the nearest window.

"Look, I had to go see her. Just make sure she was okay. I wasn't going to let her see me, but then she went and walked down a street alone. You should be glad I was fucking there. If something had happened to her, I really would have gone insane. The threat of Blaise putting a bullet in me wouldn't have been a concern. I'd have fucking done it myself." I put my elbows on the desk and leaned forward. "You can't tell me you wouldn't have done the same damn thing if someone had touched Halo."

"Halo is my wife!"

"Before she was your wife!"

"I was in love with Halo before she was my wife."

There was a pause, and I blew out a breath. "Yeah, well, I fucking love Noa." There, I'd admitted it.

I'd already faced the fact myself, but saying it to someone else made it real.

Bane's eyebrows shot up. "You admit it then?"

I rolled my eyes. "Yeah."

He sighed heavily and took off his cowboy hat and tossed it onto the chair. "Damn. That changes shit."

I watched as he walked over to the window.

"Blaise won't care that you love her. You went about all this wrong, starting with handing off the editor to the damn cartel."

Blaise Hughes might be the boss, but he wasn't going to also control who I loved. Noa had been the one thing that wasn't controlled within the family. She wasn't something I had to share. Fit into the darkness of our world. Being told that I couldn't have the one person who could calm me, make me forget the other shit, wasn't working for me.

I was glad I hadn't admitted to Bane that this hadn't been my first time to go check on her. If he knew I'd been four other times this month, then he'd really freak the hell out. I just hadn't been seen or had to kill anyone the other times. Most of those visits, she was asleep, and I sat and watched her. It had given me peace.

"I'm not worried about Blaise," I told him.

His head snapped around, and he looked at me. "You should be."

"Didn't Sebastian Shephard take his woman and run off with her? She'd been off-limits, too, and Blaise didn't kill him."

Sebastian was part of the Georgia branch, and when he'd broken command, it had spread through the family. He'd also lived, and he was engaged to the woman now.

"You're not a goddamn Shephard," Bane hissed. "Other than the Hugheses, the Shephards are the oldest line in the family. His lineage saved him. That, and his brother is a psychopath. One Blaise didn't want to kill too. Because if he'd killed Sebastian, he'd have had to kill Thatcher. The deranged son of a bitch would have burned them all to the ground in Ocala if something had happened to Sebastian. THIS"—he held out his hands—"is a completely different situation. You don't have a lethal psycho brother who is indispensable to Blaise Hughes."

There was truth to that, but I was still holding on to the fact that I would be allowed to have Noa and live.

"Is she worth losing your life over?" Bane demanded.

I stared at him for only a moment before responding honestly, "She is my life."

Bane's shoulders rose and fell as he took a deep breath and ran his hand through his hair. "All right then. What is it you want me to do?"

A grin tugged at the corners of my mouth, but I didn't dare give in and smile. Bane might have a change of heart if I pissed him off. And I did need his help.

88

"Cover for me. I need to go back and see her. Talk to her. She's hurting, and I'm the cause of it. I can't allow it to continue."

Bane's brows drew together. "And you suddenly need me to cover for you? How many times have you snuck off already to see her and not asked for a cover?"

I wasn't going to tell him that. He was already pissed. "I don't want to just watch her fucking sleep. I want to talk to her. Touch her. Fuck her. And I need more than a night to do that."

"You can't tell her anything," he snapped.

"I'm not. I just … I need her to wait for me. To know that … that I love her."

"Jesus Christ, Ransom. You had to go and decide you're in love now? This is Hawkins's first year to really understand the Santa thing and be excited about it. I can't deal with trying to keep Hughes from taking you out and enjoy my fucking holiday at the same time."

I knew she'd leave for Jellie's house tomorrow. It was what she had been doing since college. But, damn, I wanted to see her before Christmas. I didn't want her going through this holiday, thinking I didn't care. She loved this time of year. It was killing me to think she was hurting.

"I was going to go tonight," I admitted.

He shook his head. "No. After Christmas if you want my help. I can't be distracted with your shit until then. Halo has our next few days completely filled with holiday fucking cheer."

Dammit!

I needed someone to help cover for me. My going missing two days before Christmas would be noticed. There was the party at Linc's that I'd be expected to attend tomorrow, and I wasn't sure I could go see Noa and stay for only a few hours.

I was a starving man the moment I was able to touch her. I wasn't going to give a shit about anything else.

"What about Christmas night?"

"No," he replied flatly.

Fuck!

"Midnight. On the twenty-six."

The scowl on his face said he didn't like it, but that was my limit.

"Fine. Just don't get us both killed."

THIRTEEN

NOA

Standing at the center window in my living room that over-looked Bond Street, I sipped from my cup of hot cocoa and watched the cars go by. The light dusting of snow wasn't sticking, but it still gave a picturesque ambiance to the night. I'd never spent a Christmas Eve here. It was quieter than normal.

If there wasn't a world of heaviness on my chest, I'd find joy in the moment. I lifted my eyes to stare across the street at the tree lights in the apartment windows. They ranged from colorful lights to white ones, all beautiful in their own way. If I'd known I would be staying here for Christmas, I'd have gotten a tree … no, I probably wouldn't have.

Faking that much merriness was too exhausting. I was done acting as if I was okay. Which was the main reason I'd lied to Jellie and her mother about having COVID. No other explanation would have been enough for them to accept my not being there. This was going to be Zeke's first year to do Christmas with the Watts, and that was enough

of a distraction for Jellie not to be too upset about my missing it.

I'd almost packed a bag more than once today and left for
Portsmouth. But before I could even make it to the bedroom
to do so I stopped. I wasn't feeling any holiday spirit this year
and going there like this, making Melinda and Jellie worry
about me, wasn't fair. Staying in my apartment alone was
best. Even if it only added to my sadness.

The meal that Melinda had sent via a courier service was
tucked away in the refrigerator.

It wasn't the meal she'd be preparing, but it had come from
a catering service in Manhattan that offered a menu full of
holiday trimmings. The four large boxes that had arrived
seemed as if Melinda had bought me everything they had on
that list. It was sweet of her, although I'd never eat all of that.
I'd do good to taste each dish. And it had only made me feel
even guiltier about my lie. I wasn't sure what was worse—my
lying about being ill, or my being there, ten pounds lighter
than I had been at Thanksgiving, and unable to even pretend
I wasn't broken inside, causing them to worry.

I had to believe this was best. My sad presence wouldn't
dull their holiday festivities. I'd thought I was in a dark place
before, but nothing compared to where I was now.

For thirty-six hours after I'd walked away and left him on
that street, I'd worried about Ransom, if he'd gotten caught
or arrested. I waited for him to show up here. Explain things.
Make me understand why he'd shut me out. Heck, reassure
me that he was okay.

Growing desperate, I'd checked the only other access I
had to him—the distillery's Instagram.

There he was, with his brother and father, along with
their employees, raising a glass of whiskey in front of oak
barrels. He wasn't looking at the camera, but at his brother,

smiling. His cowboy hat tipped back and his arm around a woman. A stunning brunette, wearing a pair of Daisy Dukes, cowboy boots, and a Carver's Bootleg Whiskey T-shirt that was tight and cropped. She appeared to be laughing, with her eyes also on Than. As if they were sharing some inside joke.

The caption read: *Happy holidays from our family to yours. May your days be merry and your whiskey be smooth.*

It had been posted two hours before I checked it.

Ransom was, in fact, okay. He was more than okay. He was happy. Smiling. Enjoying himself. With another woman. Already. That was a blow that I hadn't been ready for, and I wasn't going to recover from it anytime soon. If I'd had a shred of hope left that what we had wasn't over, it was taken with that one photo taunting me.

I unfollowed the distillery before turning off my screen, then throwing my phone across the room. Then I'd let out a wail and crumpled to the floor to weep. I normally wasn't so dramatic, but then I'd never had my heart ripped apart like that either.

Turning away from the view, I looked over at the bookshelf that displayed my three-volume first-edition set of *Pride and Prejudice*. I'd come to accept that it was Arden who had sent them. Somewhere in his travels, he must have found them for a good price and wanted me to have them. Maybe they were an apology of sorts. If so, I wished he'd send his mother an apology. Something to ease her mind.

This Christmas wouldn't be a happy one for her either. Although his not being there wouldn't be abnormal. He never went back home for the holidays. Most of the time, he'd have his intern send wine-and-cheese baskets to his family members. I'd never questioned it because I hadn't had a relationship with my mother either.

93

Sinking down onto the sofa, I reached for the red cashmere throw that had been a gift from Melinda and was the only pop of festive color in my apartment this year. I had debated watching a Christmas movie, but decided against it and chose to play holiday music instead. The familiar twang of Dolly came over the sound system that was built into every room as she sang about hard candy. Seemed a good anthem for me this year.

With a sigh, I laid my head back and closed my eyes. I'd survive this. One day, the loss of Ransom wouldn't hurt so much. I wouldn't reach for my phone to text him something several times a day. He wouldn't be the first person I thought of when I had to share good news, a funny story, or a weird fact I'd found while doing book research.

A deep ache stretched and spread inside me instead of easing. It seemed even the idea of healing from his loss was just another layer of misery.

Even in slumber, my body sensed the danger. The other presence in the room. Knowledge that I wasn't alone. It was my racing heart that jolted me awake. Fixing my eyes on the ceiling, I tried to calm my breathing while disoriented and confused. Had I been having a nightmare?

I tried to swallow, but my mouth was dry. On instinct, I turned to get the bottle of water I left beside my bed at night.

A shadow in the darkness moved from the far-right corner and sent me bolting upright in the bed as a scream tore from my chest. The thought that I might still be dreaming, locked inside of a nightmare, crossed my mind. Regardless, this felt real. My eyes scanned quickly for anything other than a water bottle and my cell phone to use as a weapon, but went right back to the figure drawing closer. I had nothing. No way to defend myself.

I'd had nightmares since the encounter on the street with Ransom. The man he'd stabbed kept showing up in my dreams to finish what he'd started. Blood dripping from his mouth as he came to seek his vengeance. Those awful dreams hadn't felt like this, however. Even while sleeping, I had realized they weren't real. This ... this felt very real.

The sound of my heart thundered in my ears, and I scrambled back, tangling myself further in the covers.

The intruder stepped into the moonlight spilling through the curtains, and his face was illuminated. For a moment, the world froze. I stopped slapping at the covers and simply stared. No longer praying this was my imagination or a fleeting terror in my sleep. But rather the opposite.

"Ransom." His name fell from my lips in something akin to a prayer.

If this were a nightmare, it had taken a very pleasant turn.

"Who else has access to your apartment?" His husky voice filled the room, and I let out a relieved laugh.

He was here. I wasn't about to die from some stranger in the shadows. But he did hold the power to rip my heart out.

Was he here to continue causing me pain? Shred what was left of my soul?

Stiffening, I straightened, and the smile on my face vanished. He didn't get to do this. Show up in the night. Coming into my apartment, uninvited.

I had stayed up until dawn that night waiting on him. Believing that he'd come here after showing up and saving me. That he was in town to see me. He'd been following me, hadn't he? I sat on the sofa, fully dressed, and watched the sun rise through the window the following morning. But he didn't come. He vanished without another word. And then

I saw the picture of him with another woman on Instagram the next day. I had sobbed for this man, on the floor, in the fetal position.

"Is this your thing now? Ignore me and only show up for brief moments to mess with my head, then poof," I said bitterly, "disappear from my life again until you get bored and want to show back up?" I hated that my voice cracked as I said it. But in my defense, I'd just woken up, and I'd gone to sleep, crying on my pillow over the damn man.

His silence only made me angrier.

"Or were you just here to watch me sleep like some creeper, then leave without me knowing you had been here?"

The realization that a part of me wanted him to have snuck in to watch me sleep probably meant I was deranged. At least we had that in common. We both needed our sanity checked.

He had been with another woman! Her photo was on their Instagram account. She wasn't some random hookup.

"I was going to wake you," he replied. "Eventually."

I watched as he stopped at the edge of the bed, and as much as I wanted to fling myself at him, I had enough pride to jerk the covers up over my body and scoot farther away.

"No. You don't get to do this. Show up in my room at night. Show up on the street like … like Superman and save the day, then vanish!" I shouted the last part, then sucked in a breath. *And go home to another female.* I wanted to shout that at him, too, but I wasn't sure I could say it without breaking down in front of him, and I'd be damned if he saw me cry.

His deep chuckle sent a shiver through me, and, God, I really hated that. The way he could make my body react to him. I wanted to rip him from my heart. It would make my life so much easier.

"Thank fuck," he replied. "I always thought he lacked edge. Clark Kent was a pussy. I much preferred Lex Luthor.

His ruthlessness, power that was realistic, his drive, and his self-perseverance."

I frowned. "Lex Luthor was manipulative and selfish. He lacked morals," I argued. But then I was beginning to think perhaps Ransom did too. Lack morals, that was.

He tilted his head slightly and grinned wickedly. "Exactly."

Oh, how I wished that smile didn't make my heart race the way it did. But it seemed that Ransom Carver was my kryptonite. I reacted to him even when I knew the danger to my heart.

"What are you doing here, Ransom?" I demanded. I wasn't going to go back and forth with him about some stupid comic hero or villain.

"Watching you sleep. Calming the shit in my head. Soaking in your scent."

The darkness in his tone sounded tortured. Or perhaps that was my imagination. He had no reason to be tortured unless he was dealing with guilt. Man-whore guilt. I was the one who was being hurt. The one being cast aside.

"Liar," I spat. "You don't want to see me awake or asleep. Your silence made that very clear."

He leaned down just enough to reach out and grab my ankle. Before I could try and pull it free, he tugged it hard enough that it slid me to the edge of the bed. Toward him. His face was so close to mine that his breath warmed my skin.

"You're all I fucking think about from the moment I open my eyes until they finally close from exhaustion," he growled, tightening his grip on me. "Don't think for a second that this isn't killing me. It's goddamn torture. It's why I'm here, in your room, watching you. It's why I've been here four other times, doing the same thing. Needing to be near you."

I swallowed hard. Emotion caused my throat to feel thick. I didn't understand any of this. Why was *he* suffering? Why was he sneaking into my apartment at night when *he* had chosen to stay away and shut me out? Why was he with another woman?

"No! You don't!" I shouted, shoving at him, although he didn't budge. "You don't get to touch me, Ransom, or feed me your bullshit. I saw the distillery's Instagram post. The one where you're all wrapped around little Miss Daisy Dukes! While I was here, worrying about you! Afraid you'd been arrested for murder!" A tear slid down my face as my brokenness began to seep through the wall I had tried to build around it.

His brows drew together, as if he was confused, and then I watched as realization hit him. Jesus, had he already forgotten about the woman? What, had he fucked her, too, and then tossed her aside for the next in line?

He cupped the side of my face, and I jerked away from it. There was a flash of humor in his golden depths as he used the back of his finger to wipe away the tear from my cheek.

"Wrapped around her is a bit of a reach, Shakespeare," he said softly.

Did he think this was funny? I tried again to move back from him, but his hand on my ankle tightened, and he tugged me even closer.

"You're feisty when jealous."

My hand moved then, and the crack that sounded across his cheek startled me more than it did him. I froze in horror. I'd slapped him. I'd never slapped anyone in my life.

With his free hand, he grabbed my wrist and pulled my hand to his mouth. I watched, still in shock at my reaction, as he pressed a kiss to my open palm. What was he doing? I'd hit him. But he had been laughing at my being hurt. No, not hurt. I had been destroyed.

When his eyes locked back on mine, they were tender. Not the reaction to my actions one would expect.

"That woman's name is Montana Carrigan, and if my brother gets his way, it'll be Montana Carver before too long," he said. "That was the distillery's employee Christmas party. I'd been in a fucking shitty mood all day, and Than said something to set me off. I grabbed his woman, knowing it would get under his skin, and pulled her to me just as the photographer told us to raise our glasses and smile for the camera."

Oh.

I swallowed hard, and for the first time in days, breathing wasn't painful. The tightness in my chest was gone.

He dropped his head, and the brush of his lips against my shoulder made me shudder. I didn't need to be reacting to this. I shouldn't allow him to touch me. Yet my entire body felt as if he'd set it on fire from that one simple caress. That, and the relief pulsing through me. Relief that he hadn't been with someone else. He'd been having a bad day. The smile hadn't been real.

My body seemed to light up for only this man. There was that too.

Without thinking it through, I arched my neck and gave him better access as he continued a path of kisses over to my throat, nipping at my skin, then taking small licks, as if I were a treat he wanted to savor.

Even if I'd misunderstood that photo, I couldn't just let this happen. Bend to him like this. I deserved an explanation, answers. I wasn't some random booty call.

I intended to tell him just that when he snatched the covers off me and slid a hand between my thighs.

"Lie back for me," he growled near my ear, then shoved my legs open. "I've been craving the way you taste. I need you on my tongue."

Okay, so maybe we could talk after. I was panting, and the unsuccessful attempts I'd had at getting myself off lately left me unsatisfied. Ransom wouldn't leave me that way.

NO! This wasn't right. I was better than this. I wasn't like the others, where he could just snap his fingers and they'd spread their legs.

"I'm not one of your—your hookups," I said, doing my best to sound stern.

He narrowed his eyes, and his hand tightened its grip on my thigh. "No, Shakespeare, you're not. You're the reason I don't have fucking hookups anymore. I can't think about sinking my dick into any cunt but yours. Now, let me have it … please." The fierceness in his tone softened on that last word, and … well, all good intentions were gone.

He didn't … he wasn't sleeping with other women? Because of me? The surge of emotions that came with that confession made my eyes sting and my throat tighten. God, had I ever experienced a relief this powerful?

I fell back onto my elbows, then lowered myself the rest of the way.

"Fuck," he muttered as he stared down at me. His eyes drifting down my body. "I don't care what they do to me. It's worth it." His words were barely above a whisper, as if he were talking to himself.

Who was going to do something to him?

His fingers hooked the corners of my panties, and he tugged them down slowly, sliding the satin over my thighs, then calves, before discarding the fabric with a toss.

"Open your legs for me."

My body obediently did as he'd commanded. I already knew I'd regret this in the morning. But for now, I was weak. I needed him.

His nostrils flared as he lowered himself, then moved my legs onto his shoulders.

"Damn," he sighed before the first swipe of his tongue shoved away all my other thoughts.

My hands fisted in the sheets as I whimpered, wishing I were stronger. That I didn't need him so badly.

I shouldn't be doing this. He had ghosted me for an entire month. I had no reason or explanation. But he'd not been with other women. That was something. And he was here.

A deep hum vibrated in his chest as he continued to lick at me as if he couldn't get enough. My hips lifted from the mattress, and I let out a sound somewhere between a moan and a sigh. If he wanted to distract me, he was doing an excellent job.

His lips trailed kisses down the inside of my thigh as his fingers dug into my flesh, tightening his hold. "Fuuuck," he murmured. "I missed you."

The words *then why* were right there on the tip of my tongue when he flicked and sucked my clit, sending me flying off into the orgasm I'd been unsuccessful at reaching without him.

"Ransom!" I cried out as the waves of pleasure rushed over me.

"That's it. Call my name." His growl was followed by the sound of his zipper.

Panting, I lay there, watching him shove off his jeans and boxer briefs, then rip the shirt over his head, tossing it aside while climbing onto the bed and over me. I'd had my orgasm. I should be able to think clearly. Be focused on the issue, but the sight of Ransom's sculpted, tattooed chest and arms caging me in took my breath away. I said not one thing, but waited with anticipation. Knowing that once he was inside me, I wouldn't feel the ache his absence had caused. I'd be whole again.

His fingers slid into my hair and fisted, and then he pulled my head back until it was tilted up, my eyes locked on him. The rigidness of his jawline and the veins sticking out in his neck as his nostrils flared made me shiver. He looked fierce, masculine, every fantasy that I'd written on paper.

Ransom was my muse. He had been since I had been sixteen years old.

"This …" he said hoarsely, then thrust his hips and slammed into me hard. His eyes closed briefly as his breathing stuttered. "Goddamn," he murmured. "This … this is what I needed."

I could stay like this forever. Watching him in this moment of pleasure. Knowing it was me who was giving it to him. My body. He wanted me. That much I could be sure of. But my heart required more. However, right now, I was taking what he was willing to let me have. I had time. We had time. He was here with me now. I had to believe that meant the past month had a reason. One that he would explain. One that made sense. Although I already knew I'd forgive him for anything.

His gaze reminded me of a thundercloud just before the storm. There was so much in that one look that I couldn't decipher all of it. But something about it made me feel cherished. Worshipped even.

When he eased out, then back inside me, all other thoughts were gone. Just this. Us. My soul felt whole again.

FOURTEEN

NOA

The emptiness was so heavy that it was hard to breathe. I refused to open my eyes because when I did, I'd be faced with what I already knew. What I should have been prepared for but had been so wrapped up in the power of Ransom Carver that I wasn't thinking straight. He'd not explained anything. Given me no reason for his silence.

I sucked in air, and my lungs burned, but it was nothing compared to the searing in my heart.

He was gone. Without a word.

I'd fallen asleep from sheer exhaustion, wrapped in his arms. My nose buried in his neck, inhaling his scent. Lavishing in the happiness that only he brought me. Not expecting to wake up cold and alone. Desperate for a sign of hope, I listened for any sound that might tell me he was still here, although I knew, deep down, he wasn't.

There had been a darkness in his eyes last night. I wanted to believe it was guilt for having ghosted me, but I knew it was something else. Something he wouldn't share with me.

The only talking he did last night was dirty. He praised me, my body, how I made him feel. But he didn't say anything more. I had foolishly fallen asleep, thinking he'd be here when I woke up. Ready to talk.

Slowly opening my eyes, I stared at the ceiling. My eyes stung, but I refused to cry. Not again. He'd caused too many tears this past month. I'd let myself think the suffering was over last night. That he was back.

Turning over, I started to reach for my phone, thinking perhaps there was a text from him. A goodbye or explanation. But I stilled as my eyes met the dark sapphire jewel that glistened as the morning sun hit it.

What the hell was that?

Sitting up, I swung my legs off the bed and moved closer to stare down at the necklace. It was nestled in navy velvet and secured with satin. I gripped my hands tightly to my chest, backing away from it, as if it were a snake ready to strike. But perhaps a snake bite might have been less painful.

I swallowed over the familiar lump that had taken up residence in my throat.

A diamond and sapphire necklace.

I pressed a fist against my heart. I sank back down on the edge of the bed. No goodbye. No explanation. Just a gift. A ridiculously expensive one.

I winced. Although it didn't feel like a gift. He hadn't given it to me wrapped, saying, *Merry Christmas*. He'd left it beside my bed without a note. It felt like … like a payment. For what? Sex? Was that what we had become? I spread my legs, and he left me expensive jewelry to ease his conscience?

I blew out a breath and gave in to the tears. They were inevitable. Giving in now and letting them go would be easier than trying to refuse the emotion. At least I wasn't standing and wouldn't end up on the floor this time. That had been rock bottom for me. I wasn't allowing myself to go back there again.

Yet, as I assured myself of that, sobs shook my shoulders. I wanted to think he'd be back today or that he'd call me, but I already knew the truth. If he'd wanted to return to what we had been, he'd have explained his absence. He'd have stayed. Left me a letter even.

Was I expected to wait around until he had time to show up again? Or was my necklace a parting gift?

I glared hatefully at the offending item. There was no telling the price tag on it. The case it was in said *Harry Winston*. Of course it was. I'd never even bought myself something from there. The damn thing probably needed its own insurance policy. I'd mail the thing to him if it didn't cost so much. I would just shove it at him the next time he showed up … if there was a next time. I could use it to slap his face instead of my hand.

Letting out a frustrated growl, I shot up off the bed and slammed the lid to the jewelry box closed.

"Damn you, Ransom," I muttered at the item, then snatched up my phone while wiping my wet cheeks with my hand and headed for the kitchen.

I was almost to my coffee maker when my phone rang, and like an idiot, I flipped it over to look at it while my heart picked up its pace. *Unknown* flashed on the screen, and I paused before hitting Answer.

"Hello," I said, trying to tamp down the hope that this was Ransom blossoming in my chest.

No one said anything. I pulled the phone back and glanced at it to be sure the call hadn't been dropped. It was active. Someone was on the other line. Or maybe it was a spam call and the recording hadn't started yet.

I waited. A minute went by as I stared at the clock on the microwave. Nothing. I looked again, and the call still hadn't ended.

"Hello?" I repeated, knowing I should hang up, but my stupid need for this to be Ransom stopped me.

"It's your fault," the same voice that had called before said.

Frowning, I started to ask what was, but the call ended. Slowly, I laid the phone down on the counter and moved away from it, as if it were the cause of the odd calls I'd received.

My phone lit up again, and I started to take another step back, as if it were going to harm me, but Jellie's name appeared, along with a text. Letting out a sigh, I moved back to the counter and slid my finger over the screen to read what she had said.

> Jellie: I asked for one thing. ONE SIMPLE thing. The sandcastle Jellycat. I even sent him a picture of it! It wasn't a freaking diamond or designer purse. IT WAS A JELLYCAT! Why is he so slow? What do I need to do to this man in order to get the point across when I want something? Do you know what he got me? A toaster! He bought me a freaking toaster. Apparently, I said it was cute or something! And it is! But I don't want a toaster for Christmas!!! What am I, eighty?

You'd have thought by now that he'd know that those silly stuffed animals that shared her name was all it took to make her happy. He'd probably paid too much for whatever cute toaster he bought. I was a little curious about what kind it was and what it looked like. But I didn't ask for a picture just yet. She wasn't done venting.

106

> Me: Men. They need more than pictures. They need you to tell them things.

As if I was one to give any advice on men.

Her dots appeared as she began typing, and I set the phone back down, knowing this was going to be a long one. Moving over to the coffee maker, I started to make a cup while I gave her time to respond. Once I had it going, I glanced back at my screen to see that she'd sent another one.

> Jellie: He is mad now! Because I wanted the Jellycat! He said I was impossible to please! SERIOUSLY! I am moving to Manhattan. We will be roommates and grow old together. Screw men! We don't need them. You just have to buy me the damn Jellycat I want when it's a holiday.

I'd needed a distraction, and Jellie was good at that.

> Me: Deal. But you're not getting my office. You'll have to take the guest bedroom.

I waited for her response, doing my best to focus on this and not Ransom. Or his damn necklace.

The phone started to ring, and Jellie's name lit up the screen.

I hit Answer and put it on speaker.

"Yesss?" I drawled out.

"That is the smallest room in your apartment! You would really stick me in that tiny bedroom?! I thought we were best friends?"

"Hmm ... we are, but my love only goes so far," I replied, then took a sip of my coffee.

"You're an evil woman. How are we friends?" she shot back at me.

"Because you love me and can't live without me."

She sighed heavily. "Yes, and the two people I love most suck. Unless you will buy me the sandcastle Jellycat."

I chuckled and set my cup down on the counter before reaching for a gluten-free bagel that I'd bought from the deli yesterday.

"Why can't you buy the thing?" I asked.

"Because I need a story to go with it!"

"A story?" I asked, confused.

"Yes, a story. All my Jellycats have a story. Who gave it to me and when. Like the Christmas tree one Mom sent me when she found out I didn't have a tree up last year in my apartment. Or the to-go coffee one you gave me for my birthday last year. And when his ass ever gets around to proposing, I want the engagement ring Jellycat! If he forgets that, I am turning him down."

I walked over to the fridge and got out the butter. "I say you let this one mistake slide. He's a guy. He might have thought you had enough Jellycats and didn't want any more."

"I SENT HIM A PICTURE!" she yelled.

"And like I said, he's a guy."

"Whatever. I still may leave him and move in with you. Even if you are only giving me the tiny room."

I knew she'd never do it. She loved Zeke and Boston.

"Sure you will," I replied.

"So, how are you feeling?" she asked. "You were missed here. I think Birch bitched about it the most. If he said, 'Noa would have loved this,' one time, he said it a million. It was verging on weird. My brother may have a thing for you."

I doubted it, but even if he did, that was never happening. Not just because Ransom had broken me, but Birch was part of the only family I had ever really had. I wasn't messing that up.

"I'm feeling better. Tell me what all I missed," I said, wanting to get the topic off me.

Taking my phone over to the sofa, I sat down and listened as she chatted on about the Watts family Christmas, thankful for something to fill the silence.

FIFTEEN
NOA

The overcast sky matched my mood. Tugging the belt of my navy Burberry nylon hooded raincoat tighter, I shivered. Hopefully, it didn't rain, but if it did, I was prepared. I hated carrying umbrellas and much preferred a hooded jacket. However, they didn't help much if it was a downpour. I might regret not taking an umbrella. The sky did not look promising. It wasn't cold enough for snow—at least I could be thankful for that.

My editor had called this morning, and I should be inside, writing. She was getting stressed about my deadline. The offices were closed until the second week in January, but she was still working at home and anxious for me to send her more words.

This was our first time working together on a book, and I knew she wanted to make a good impression. I didn't want to take that from her, but I was blocked, and if I stayed in that apartment one more minute, I was going to go crazy. I needed to get out and walk. Clear my head. Possibly get inspiration for the next chapter because, right now, I had no clue what was going to happen next.

"Noa Raines," a female voice said, and I paused.

Normally, if anyone noticed me in the city, they called me Juliette Romeo. Not my real name. When I turned around, a sense of foreboding began to sink over me.

An older woman with silver streaks in her once-dark-brown bob—wearing round black-framed glasses, dressed in a pair of tan slacks and an oversize cream cable-knit sweater beneath her heavy wool coat—stood several feet away from me. She studied me as closely as I was her.

Who was she? Something about the woman was familiar, but I couldn't place it.

"Yes?" I finally replied when she said nothing more.

Her eyes flickered with unease, and then they narrowed. Her expression took on an edge. She looked fierce, and whatever had caused her anger was directed at me.

When had I pissed off someone's grandmother?

"Where is my Arden?" she demanded with a sharper tone than before.

It was then that I realized what I'd found familiar … Arden's eyes. This was his mother. He'd never even shown me a photo of his parents, but I could see it. Even her glare was like his.

"I don't know," I replied honestly.

I wasn't about to tell her my theory of the mob. If he had left willingly, then he was an even bigger asshole than I'd realized. I'd heard that his parents didn't believe he would just leave and were looking for him. But until now, I hadn't thought too deeply about it. I'd been wrapped up in my own problems.

It was obvious his mother was hurting and desperate for answers. But I didn't have any answers. For her or me.

"I don't believe you," she snapped. "You were engaged. The PI I hired found that out. Arden never told us about you." She said it as if that were my fault. Her son had kept us a secret for his reasons, not mine. "Why is that? What was it that he had to be ashamed of about you?"

That didn't sting. I knew her words were those of a mother in pain and she was lashing out, but nothing she said to me would actually do any damage. Arden hadn't held that power over me.

"He didn't tell anyone," I said. And that was the truth.

How the PI had found out, I didn't know. It was clearly a very good one. Maybe he could locate Arden. I hoped so, for his mother's sake.

She pointed a finger at me accusingly. "He didn't want to tell people." She seethed as if she knew some secret I was keeping. "That made you retaliate! He hurt you, and you are a spoiled diva who expects to get her way. He didn't give you what you wanted, and you got rid of him! I know you did this!"

That was entirely more energy and planning than I'd ever put into anything with Arden. She wasn't going to find him on that path. I'd had nothing to do with his disappearance. I started to shake my head when the door to my apartment building opened, and Wayne—one of three security guards who alternated working the front entrance—stepped outside. He was older, possibly sixty, but built like a linebacker with broad shoulders. His slick, bald head made him appear more intimidating than he actually was.

"Is there a problem, Ms. Romeo?" he asked me, his gaze flickering from me to the other woman, then back again.

The woman's jaw was jutted out, and her hands were clasped tightly, pressing close to her stomach. I felt bad for her. No mother should be put through this.

"Uh, no," I said to Wayne, trying to attempt a reassuring smile.

He looked back at the other woman. "Doesn't seem very friendly out here," he drawled, turning his gaze back to me.

Did he think I needed protecting from a woman more than twice my age?

Come on, Wayne. She's not about to tackle me to the ground or take my purse and run.

"You know something. And my PI is suddenly missing. I don't care how much money those trashy books of yours has made you." She raised her eyebrows at me with an air of haughtiness. "I will find out what you've done! You will pay!" Her voice rose enough to draw attention from others passing by on the street.

I opened my mouth to defend myself, but stopped before I did. She didn't want to hear my truth. She needed a lead to her son, and believing I was it was all she had to cling to. When I said nothing more, Wayne stepped between us to block her view of me. I looked from him, then leaned to the side slightly to see her spin around and stalk away.

"She don't seem real sane, Ms. Romeo," Wayne said, drawing my attention back to him.

"Her son left town with nothing but a note. She's upset, and she wants answers," I explained.

His brows drew together. "Not an excuse," he said with a shake of his head. "No need to go taking it out on you. You've not done a thing."

I smiled at Wayne, although I didn't feel like it. The interaction had bothered me, but I didn't want him to know that.

"It's fine. I'm fine," I reassured him. "His leaving was odd and hard to believe for everyone. It wasn't like him. I'm the only lead she thinks she has." And I did feel bad for her.

113

"Might be best if you came on back inside for now," he suggested.

"No," I said. I had to get out. "I need the fresh air and some time to think about my words before going back up to work."

He crinkled his nose and looked around. "There isn't anything real fresh about this air," he pointed out, causing a small laugh to bubble out of me. He was right, of course.

"A walk will do me good. Even with the questionable air quality."

The corner of his mouth quirked. "All right then. But keep your eyes open. Stay alert."

I nodded once. "Will do."

Glancing around him one more time to see that Arden's mother was no longer in sight, I sighed a breath of relief and gave Wayne a small wave before heading in the opposite direction.

SIXTEEN
RANSOM

Pacing, I stared down at my phone, watching the tracker I'd put in Noa's phone and the lining of her wallet. After Wayne had called me to tell me about the visitor she had on the street, I'd escaped to my room so that I could keep tabs on her location.

Fucking Arden was a pain in the ass. Causing more problems. Why couldn't he disappear properly?! Dammit!

We'd shut up the PI, but I did have a line I wasn't going to cross, and torturing his mother was on the other side of it. I had to find a way to get her to stop her pursuit of him without doing any bodily harm.

She'd been walking in the direction of her apartment earlier, and she should be there by now.

Zooming in, I looked to see the name of where she had stopped. Swanky Brew—must be a coffee shop. So far, on her outing, she had stopped at a bookstore, two boutiques, Dainty Cakes—which I'd looked up online, and it was a cupcake bakery that had gluten-free items—and now coffee.

Part of me was glad she was out of the apartment, but then there was the other part that liked her to stay where I could see her. That was selfish, but my rationality was getting more questionable, the longer I was kept from Noa. If I turned into a full-blown psycho, then it was Linc's fault—no, make that Blaise's fault. It would be all their damn fault.

The fucking image of the Ken Doll that wanted what was mine taunted me. I'd blocked his number from her phone, but what if she'd figured it out and unblocked him? Or he could call from another line. I didn't want to think that she would spend time with that douchebag. Especially since we'd been together three nights ago.

She hadn't said she loved me, but the way she'd looked at me when I was inside her the other night sure as hell felt like it. I had to leave her while she was sleeping, but it was just easier that way. I wasn't sure I could do it if she asked me not to go. She had no idea what she would be asking of me, and I was starting to think telling her no would be something I couldn't do. So, I had slipped away while she slept, but only after lying there, watching her, for three hours. Embedding the sight of her, the smell, the way she felt, curled up against me, into my damn soul. Something to replay when I was going fucking crazy from having to stay away from her.

The necklace I'd left wasn't an exact replica of the one she described in her book, but when I had gone looking for a necklace like it, I'd found that one instead. It was elegant, beautiful, and flawless. I'd wanted it for her. I hadn't left a note because, like the other gifts I'd sent her, it held significance from one of her books. I wanted her to realize it and see the meaning behind each gift.

I was regretting not leaving a note now. Unlike the books that she'd displayed in her living room, the necklace she'd not even taken out and examined. She'd closed it, cursed at me, and later shoved it in her closet. I'd replayed the video feed of her doing it at least a dozen times, trying to figure out what had triggered her temper. I still wasn't sure why she was so upset about the necklace, and I couldn't fucking get away and go fix whatever had upset her. I was under a damn microscope.

Unfortunately, Linc had called a meeting that I didn't make it to because it was at seven the next morning. I was driving back from the private airstrip in Jackson when the summons came. This was where having Bane cover for me went into play. He did what I'd asked, and it saved my ass, but Linc had been more diligent in keeping tabs on me since then.

Bane's lie about my going to a strip club in Jackson and waking up in a hotel room, hungover, with two strippers should have been sufficient, but something about it had made Linc suspicious. Since then, he'd had me being watched too damn closely. I wouldn't have thought he'd question it, coming from Bane, but he had, and I was having to wait the shit out.

She was moving again. Must have gotten a cup to go. I stopped and leaned against the doorframe leading into my en suite while I watched as she headed in the direction of her apartment. She'd had a good outing, and if the tracker was any indication, there had been no other issues since Arden's mother had shown up to threaten her.

My head snapped up to glare at the door when a knock sounded on it. Who the fuck was bothering me? I was busy, dammit.

"Ransom," Forge called. "We got business to handle. You, me, and Oz."

Fucking hell.

"What is it?" I asked, not wanting to stop watching Noa until she was safely back at her place.

"Does it matter? I don't fuckin' know. Oz just told me to get you and meet him in the Escalade in ten."

With a sigh, I watched as she drew closer to the building, then shot Wayne a text to let me know when she was safely inside before shoving my phone back in my pocket. I wasn't sure how long we'd be gone, and I wasn't going without a way to check on her. Going to the closet, I took out my black leather jacket, then unzipped the inside hidden pocket and slipped the phone inside.

As much as I didn't want to be taken away from my freedom to watch Noa, a little violence might help ease all the fucking tension churning inside me. Hopefully, there would be some torture involved.

Climbing into the passenger side of the Escalade, I glanced over at Oz, who was looking at the GPS on his phone in the driver's seat.

"What are we handling?" I asked.

"Got a few overdue debts. Linc said to go collect," he replied.

Oz was the family's bookie in Mississippi. This was a regular thing, but especially after the holidays. Folks overspent, and when it was time to pay up, they were broke. I almost felt sorry for some of them, but Oz vetted most everyone he let into his ring, and they passed the credit test. The stupid bastards should be smarter with their cash.

"We starting low going high, or vice versa?" I asked.

Typically, we went to the debts that were smaller and made our way up to the heavy ones. It got messier, the more money they owed, and once we got blood on our hands, we liked to go on home and clean up.

"Eh, they're all pretty fucking high this time. Too many upsets on Thanksgiving weekend. A lot of fuckers lost big money," he replied. "Linc let it slide until after Christmas, but the grace period is over."

Thanksgiving Day, there had been three upsets in college ball and three in NFL games. Most of those placing bets had done so in hopes of extra cash for the holidays, but joke was on them. I never asked about the profit and loss within our bookmaking branch of the family unless we had to funnel money through the distillery. Then I wanted details.

The door behind Oz opened, and Forge climbed inside.

"Sorry, had to take a shit," he said, pulling out his revolver and laying it on the seat beside him. "You got an extra .38? I could only find one," he said, reaching for his seat belt.

"Under your seat," Oz said without looking up from his phone.

"Thank fuck," Forge muttered and bent to reach under and get the case with the extra firearms.

"All right, might as well hit up the former NFL star first. Get it over with," Oz said as he hit the button that lifted the door to the garage.

"Not Draughn," Forge said. "Not again."

Rock Draughn was our local celebrity. He lived in Jackson now that he was retired with the baby momma he had finally settled down with three years ago. He was a Hall of Famer in the NFL. Unfortunately, this wasn't the first time we'd had to go collect from him.

"Get over your man crush," Oz drawled. "Bastard has an addiction, and I don't mind feeding it as long as he pays what he owes. He bet on his former team Thanksgiving and got fucked. Time he pays up."

119

"Fuck," Forge groaned. "You threatened to puzzle his fingers last time. Please tell me you were full of shit. His hand is legendary."

Oz glanced up at him through the rearview mirror. "I'm never full of shit. He doesn't pay, then I am blamed. And his wife's Instagram shows they were in Hawaii on a private yacht the week of Christmas. He needs to learn to manage his money properly. I don't give one flying fuck about his hand. I care about the fifty grand he owes us."

I let out a low whistle and shook my head. "Damn, dude should have married money, not some hot-piece-of-ass cheerleader."

"No shit," Oz agreed.

"What if he pays up? Do we leave the hand alone?" Forge asked.

Oz cut his eyes back to the rearview mirror again. "Did you not hear the part about the yacht? Fucker hasn't paid because he's broke. He'll need time to sell something. And if that is what he tells me, which it will be, then his fingers are going between the nails."

Forge let out a groan and leaned back dejectedly in his seat. "Fuck."

I grinned and shook my head. "If I hadn't witnessed you eating pussy like a damn addict, I'd think you wanted his cock in your mouth."

Oz chuckled beside me, but said nothing.

"Nah, I wouldn't take a cock in my mouth even if it was gonna save the golden grip."

"It stopped being golden when arthritis set in," I told him. "Hence his retirement."

Forge stuck a cigarette between his lips and leaned forward to pull the lighter out of his pocket. "Yeah, but it's still the hand that's thrown six hundred and twenty-two touchdowns."

"Brady broke that record," Oz said.

"Doesn't matter," Forge told him. "Draughn is a Mississippi boy. That should mean something."

Oz smirked as we pulled through the security gate and onto the main road.

"If I make my point with his left hand, will that shut you the fuck up?"

Forge's brows lifted as hope lit his eyes. We were still discussing the fact that Oz was going to put a Hall of Famer's hand on a wooden board with nails between each finger, then slam a hammer into the side of them, breaking them all at once and leaving them unnaturally bent. But since it wasn't his former famous hand, then Forge was okay with it.

"Seriously?" he asked.

Oz nodded. "Yeah. But if you say one more goddamn word about his fucking hand, I will break both set of fingers."

I felt the hidden phone in my pocket vibrate and clenched my hands to keep from checking it. Wayne was most likely letting me know that Noa was back safe, but I wanted to see the reassurance for myself. Hopefully, these bastards paid up, and we wouldn't have to spend time making them wish they had.

SEVENTEEN
NOA

This was not a night that I wanted to go out on. Especially in Manhattan. The tourists had started pouring in the day after Christmas, and as the week went on, it had just gotten worse. All leading up to the streets packed with over one million people in and around Times Square. While the square was almost three miles away, the nightlife in NoHo brought its own crowd.

But since I'd lied about COVID and I had extreme guilt about that, I couldn't tell Jellie no when she told me they would be in town tonight. Zeke had a friend with reservations for the VIP party at the Marriott Marquis with terrace viewing of the ball drop. Which was not the easiest place to get into on New Year's Eve. The hotel had an excellent view of the ball drop without being on the packed streets. She had claimed one of those VIP tickets for me and not really given me an option to say no.

They weren't staying at the hotel itself because it was booked solid. But they were staying a few blocks away in

Midtown. She'd wanted me to come there, but it was either walk the two miles and get ready there or get ready at home and take the subway. Traffic would be so congested, so taking a taxi was out of the question. I'd decided to just get dressed here and take the subway.

Under different circumstances, I would have cause to celebrate. I'd managed to write fifteen thousand words this week. It had been a struggle to get going at first because of Ransom's middle-of-the-night booty call and then return to complete silence. Once the words had started coming though, they had begun to flow. The angst in this one was unlike anything I'd written before, and I was excited about that. Writing heart-wrenching scenes helped me express my own pain, and I was finding that it was therapeutic.

Checking myself one more time in my full-length mirror, I decided that this dress was the best option for tonight. Jellie had said to wear something gold or black, but I didn't own anything gold. I had some black dresses, but none that felt festive. She was going to have to be happy with silver. I'd bought it for a gala last December that raised money for Project Night Night—a charity that provided a new book, a security blanket, and a stuffed animal to homeless children under the age of twelve. Although I didn't much care for galas, I'd gone to that one because Project Night Night was one of the charities I donated to monthly. Although I hadn't been a homeless child, I'd loved to read, and thanks to the school library, I could feed my love. It was an escape from my reality. Books had saved me. I knew the power they held.

Walking over to the dresser, I picked up the earrings I'd chosen for tonight and put them on. My eyes kept going back to the drawer where I'd put the necklace Ransom had left me. I hated everything that necklace represented. But it was the most gorgeous piece of jewelry I'd ever owned. Even if I did want to wear it, I couldn't put that on and ride the subway. That was asking to get mugged. The thing probably cost twenty-five grand or something ridiculous like that. If Ransom ever showed back up, I intended to shove it at him and tell him to leave.

I'd actually imagined the scene several times. Mostly while standing in the shower, crying.

The sound that alerted me that someone was downstairs, wanting to get in to see me, went off, and I paused, frowning in its direction, then quickly made my way toward the camera to see who it was.

Who would be here on a night like tonight?

I stopped walking before I reached it when Thurston's face popped into my head. I did not want to deal with him. And I was not about to bring him along with me. He'd been quiet, and I had been thankful for that. I hoped he had gotten the message.

The sound went off again. Would Jellie have come here? Why would she do that though? She hated the subway, and she wouldn't want to walk the two miles. But then she might think I would back out at the last minute, so she could have braved the subway for that.

Reluctantly, I went to see who it was, just in case it was her.

The sight of Birch standing outside my building—wearing a slim-fit charcoal-gray suit with a black shirt and his normally slightly wavy, dark hair slicked back in a low ponytail—was not what I'd expected to find.

"What the hell?" I muttered, then hit the talk button.

"Are you lost?" I asked him.

He smirked. "I was in the neighborhood."

Sure he was. Birch hated Manhattan.

"Uh-huh."

"I'm here to escort you, Ms. Romeo," he replied, grinning now.

This was Jellie's doing.

"Your sister does realize that I live here. I use the subway often," I replied.

His shocked expression was fake. "You don't say?"

Laughing, I pressed the entrance button, and he reached to open the door as it unlocked for him.

"I believe Wayne is still on duty. Tell him you're here for me."

He turned back to the camera and saluted me before disappearing inside.

I walked back to the bedroom to get my cell phone and text my best friend. I hadn't even known Birch was coming tonight. But then I had a feeling she hadn't told me on purpose so she could blindside me with his showing up to escort me. At least it was Birch and not some annoying hookup.

Picking up my phone, I found our text thread and began typing out my response to this as I went back to the front door to open it for Birch.

> Me: Thank you, Mommy, for my bodyguard.

Her dots were almost immediate. Birch had probably already texted her, and she was on her phone.

> Jellie: Anytime, baby girl.

Rolling my eyes, I started to respond when the doorbell rang. Closing the short distance, I unbolted it and opened it up to see my best friend's older brother. I'd only seen him looking like this once, and that was for a cousin's wedding I'd attended with Jellie as her plus-one several years ago. He cleaned up nicely.

"You didn't think you were going to skip getting to be in my presence the entire holiday season, did you?" he asked, holding out his arms, as if to display himself, before winking and walking inside. "Lucky for you, I'm a thoughtful kinda guy. I'd never make you suffer like that."

I closed the door behind him, then turned to see him checking the place out. He'd been here before, but that was to help me move in. I'd done a lot since then.

"Where is Titan while you're in the Big Apple for New Year's?" I asked, crossing my arms over my chest.

He swung his gaze back to mine. "At my parents'."

"Melinda is letting him stay there without you?"

"He worked his charm and claimed her heart. I taught him how to reel in the ladies. She might not give him back. If there's a custody case in court, I'll need you as a witness."

A real laugh bubbled out of me. The sound was almost foreign. I'd not laughed in a while. It was nice.

"As much as I love you and all, Melinda trumps you. I'd totally vouch for her."

He rolled his eyes skyward and sighed. "It's the hair, isn't it? The ponytail is affecting my magnetism."

I shrugged. "It may have a touch to do with it, but even still, Melinda wins."

"Damn," he muttered with a sigh. "In that case, you are no longer invited to our judicial battle."

"Good."

He grinned, then did a quick sweep of my outfit. "You look hot for someone who just survived pretend COVID."

I paled slightly, then frowned. "What's that supposed to mean?" Dammit, my voice wavered. I hated lying, and being called out on it was bad.

He tilted his head to the side and cocked an eyebrow at me. "That's what I thought. Whatever was wrong with you at

Thanksgiving is still wrong now. Who is he? Where do I find him? I'll take Titan and go beat his ass."

Stiffening, I straightened my shoulders and shook my head. "I don't know what you're talking about. I was sick. I've lost weight."

His expression didn't change. "Yeah, and heartbreak will do that to you. Or so I've heard. Never given anyone the power to break mine." He took a step toward me and then held out his elbow. "Come on. Let's get our asses to Midtown, and you can tell me all about it on the way."

"There is nothing to tell," I told him.

"Uh-huh," he replied. "You keep on wasting your breath with the lies. I'll have a name before the night is over."

No, he wouldn't. And not just because I was trying to cover up my COVID lie either. But because Birch had no idea that the ass he was threatening to beat was one born into a crime family. I had to convince him I was fine. He needed to let this theory, which was eerily accurate, go. For his own good.

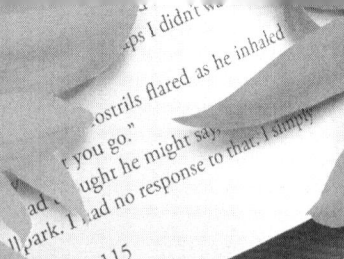

ostrils flared as he inhaled

r you go.

ught he might say,

ugh I didn't w

ad,

ballpark. I had no response to that, I simply

the

115

EIGHTEEN
NOA

The DJ currently doing a set had just put on "I Gotta Feeling" by the Black Eyed Peas, and Jellie squealed, grabbing Zeke's hand to pull him out onto the floor to dance. The open bar was her best friend tonight. I'd lost count of the lemon drops she'd had. The noise and energy inside and outside on the terrace were doing a good job of distracting me.

"You wanna dance?" Birch asked as he held out the whiskey sour he'd gone to get at the bar for me.

"Nope," I replied, taking it. "I've not had enough alcohol yet."

He chuckled. "All right, but if you don't drink faster, I'm going to give that hot little redhead who keeps eyeing me a chance."

I nodded my head in her direction. "Please, go dance with her. I'm just fine. You're not required to babysit me."

"You're why I'm here," he said with a shrug, then took a drink of his whiskey. "You missed the family Christmas.

Finton and I agreed something was up with you, and I volunteered to come check things out."

Although there was nothing either of them could do to help, it made my throat tighten with emotion.

Growing up without anyone to care about me or be concerned about my well-being had deprived me of the feeling of belonging and family. The day I met Jellie Watts, my world changed. I'd not just gotten a best friend, but her family as well. I knew they cared about me, but hearing Birch say that he and Finton had discussed me and wanted to check on me was special. Something I never imagined I'd have.

Birch set his glass on the table and leaned closer to me as he studied my face. "Are you about to cry?" he asked.

I scowled as I sniffled. "Shut up."

"Noa," he said, lowering his voice. "Please tell me you're not fucking pregnant."

I let out a startled laugh. "No! Why would you say that?"

He leaned back some, looking relieved. "Because you were tearing up over Fint and me worrying about you."

I held up my glass. "This is my second whiskey sour. If I was pregnant, I would not be drinking."

His shoulders relaxed, and he nodded. "Right. I don't know any pregnant women, so I forget the things to look for. I just thought emotional and pregnancy," he said, then picked up his glass and took a drink.

I watched as he glanced over at the redhead again. He was right. She was definitely looking over here. I grinned into my glass. I'd never thought of Birch, or Finton for that matter, like that. But that didn't mean they weren't handsome. Both were single men with solid careers. The redhead could do worse. Although I knew Birch wasn't interested in anything more than sex. Hopefully, that was all she had in mind too. That, and a dance partner to ring in the new year with.

The redhead picked up her martini glass and started in our direction. Seemed she wasn't waiting any longer for him to approach her. I'd never had that kind of confidence. It was admirable. I might use her as inspiration for my next heroine.

"Your hottie is headed this way," I said under my breath since Birch was now looking out the tall glass windows overlooking Times Square.

His eyes shot back to mine, and I nodded my head slightly in her direction, trying not to be obvious.

"The redhead?" he asked.

"Yep."

He smirked, looking smug. "It's the ponytail. You might not love it, but it reels them in."

I bit back a laugh and relaxed in my chair to watch this play out. It might be something juicy to tuck away for a scene one day. The redhead glanced from Birch to me, then smiled. Up close, she didn't appear as confident. I was sensing nerves, yet here she came anyway. Damn, I wished I had that kind of courage. He'd better be nice to this one. I liked her.

When she reached us, she flashed a smile at Birch as he turned to fully face her, but her gaze moved back to me.

"Uh, whew, okay," she said, followed by a shaky giggle. "Sorry. I worked up the courage to come over here, and now I am awestruck, and words aren't coming."

I glanced at Birch, waiting for him to say something to make her feel better.

He leaned his head slightly toward her. "It's hot," he assured her, then winked.

Her brows drew together, as if she was confused. She looked up at him, then turned to look back at me. Was she making sure we weren't together? Did I need to make that clear?

"I'm just a really big fan. I've read your books so many times that I had to buy new copies because the covers were looking worn," she blurted.

Oh! OH! She was here for me.

I sat up straighter this time and plastered on my Juliette Romeo smile. The one that hid all my insecurities.

"I have a copy in my purse at the coat check. I … I, uh, carry a book with me when I go places in case I want to go hide and read."

I could not look at Birch. If I did, I was afraid I would laugh. What this must be doing to his ego.

"It's nice to meet you," I told her. "I'm honored."

She blushed and then scrunched her nose. "Is it bad for me to ask if you'd sign my book? I mean, I know you're out, having a good time with friends, and if that is—"

I stopped her before she continued. "It is never bad to ask me to sign your book. You read my words and loved them so much that you carry them with you. I'd be upset if I didn't get to sign it."

She let out a relieved sigh. "Thank you."

She glanced at Birch again, as if making sure he was still there and not sure what to do about him. I still thought she might be interested, but my guess was, she thought he was with me.

"I'll, uh, be right back."

"No worries," I told her. "Take your time."

She nodded, then turned to walk back toward where the coat check was located, and I swung my gaze over to grin as I took a drink from my glass.

"Ouch," I said teasingly.

He let out a disbelieving chuckle. "That was a fucking first."

131

I just bet it was. "If it makes your ego feel any better, I still think she is interested in you. But she is unsure about us," I said. "I can clear that up if you'd like me to."

He shook his head. "No, I don't think I can move past the fact that I just got passed over, and it wasn't even for another dude."

As I sat in the middle of all of this, actually enjoying the humor of it all, my mind instantly went to Ransom. I wanted to tell him about it. He'd think it was hilarious. The itch to grab my phone and text him sent the sadness barreling through the walls I'd tried to erect to hold it back—at least for tonight.

"She's a gorgeous female, and she reads. You sure you want to pass that up? You normally just go for the ones who overuse filler words while talking about their latest visit to a photo shoot in Paris." That was a little harsh, but my mood had sunk.

He shook his head as the corners of his mouth curled up. "If she's reading your shit, then maybe I do want to hook up with her. She's got some excellent pointers from that naughty imagination of yours." He took a drink, then glanced back at me with a confused look. "What the fuck are filler words?"

After Amelia, the redhead, took her signed book and left to go back to her table—because Birch had decided to pass on her, which I thought was stupid—I went to the restroom. Jellie had kept Zeke on the floor for the next two songs, and I didn't think they'd be coming back to sit anytime soon. I needed a quieter moment, and a stall in the restroom seemed like the only place I'd find that here. Plus, it would give Birch a chance to find a female for the night. I was sure his sitting with me was hindering that.

When I turned the corner to the stairs, it was already easier to breathe. I wasn't one for crowds, and although this was nothing like what was happening outside on the street below, it was still a lot of peopling for me. I was unsure if the restroom was on this level, but exploring didn't bother me. It gave me more of a break.

When I passed an older lady, I asked her if the restroom was this way, and she nodded but kept walking. Not very friendly, but again, I didn't mind looking for it. No rush. I didn't actually have to pee. Pausing to decide if she had come from the left or the right, I went left since it had more lighting and the darker set of stairs seemed less likely to be the way to go.

I'd barely taken three steps when a hand covered my mouth as an arm wrapped around my waist …

NINETEEN
RANSOM

"Easy, Shakespeare," I whispered close to her ear, and the struggle she'd immediately put up ceased, making it easier to pull her into the hotel employee elevator.

Once the doors closed, I uncovered her mouth.

"What ..." she said, sounding breathless as she stared up at me, wide-eyed, but it was only the briefest moment before her hand slapped my chest with what was probably meant to be a hard hit. "You scared me to death!"

Well, she shouldn't have been out with a man at a fucking New Year's Eve party.

"I told you I didn't share," I said, gripping her waist and tugging her closer to me as she tried to step back.

She was mad at me. I'd hurt her. But she didn't belong here with some other fucking man.

A sharp, short laugh that held no humor came from her pretty lips, and again, she tried to free herself from my hold. It was pointless. I wasn't letting go of her. I'd just put my life at risk to come get her.

Wayne's call about a man going up to her apartment, dressed in a goddamn suit, had sent me speeding to the airport without any plan or thought. I'd already been in the private plane I'd paid too much for at the last minute when Wayne sent a text, saying that they had left together and, in his words, *She was dressed up real nice.*

"Share? I'm sorry, but sharing requires you having something and letting someone else use it. You don't have me, Ransom. You shut me out. You fucked me and left. No explanation, no goodbye, just an expensive piece of jewelry, like I was some high-end prostitute!" she shouted, then started fighting to get free of me again.

The doors opened behind her, and I looked at them, then back down at her. "Don't cause a scene. Be a good girl." It wasn't a demand—at least I hadn't meant for it to sound like one. It was a request. "You can yell at me and hit me some more when we get to the privacy of our room."

She frowned, then seemed caught off guard. "What room? Here?"

I nodded.

"There're no available rooms here. This night has probably been booked solid since last New Year's Eve."

It had been, but the right amount of money could get people to do things. Like give up their suite with a view of the ball drop and move to another hotel. Also ten cases of Carver's Bootleg Whiskey Exclusive Label could make things happen. Like the helicopter that I took from the airport to the helipad closest to the hotel. The fucking traffic was insane, and I hadn't had time to sit in a goddamn car while Noa was on a date.

Placing my hand on her lower back, I led her out of the elevator and around to the hotel's main elevators, which would take us to our room. When we stepped inside the next elevator, I took the key card and tapped the small black reader before pressing our floor number, then glanced over at her. Those eyes I loved so fucking much widened in surprise.

"You do have a room," she said as her eyes flickered up to mine.

I nodded.

"How?"

Smirking, I licked my bottom lip and let my gaze drift down her body. The silver satin material had a shimmer to it as it clung to her body. Fuck, she was breathtaking. But she'd dressed like this for another man. Because of it, he might not get to live. The rage slowly burning under my controlled surface was getting stronger, the more I thought about it.

"Did he kiss you?" I asked through clenched teeth.

"Who?" she asked.

"Your fucking date, Shakespeare. Did he kiss you?" I asked slower and with more threat in my tone than I wanted to use around her.

She crossed her arms beneath her tits, causing them to jiggle. "Since I don't have a date, I still do not know who you are referring to," she snapped at me angrily.

Nice try, Shakespeare, but I saw him.

I'd memorized his face. He'd pay for touching her.

"I watched you for thirty-five minutes before you left the table and came searching for the restroom. Don't lie to me."

Her full lips pursed, and she lifted her chin slightly. I loved the way she tasted right below there; the smooth, creamy skin on her neck tasted like fucking peaches.

"Did you now? Tell me, Ransom, why is it that you can't seem to text me, or call me, or explain to me why you have chosen to ignore me, yet you can track me down at a VIP party that is very difficult to get into?" She paused and pointed back at the closed elevator doors. "There were celebrities at

136

that thing. The tickets weren't easy to get, and like this hotel, it was sold out. But not for you. Because you can get in any-where you want, but you can't send me one goddamn text!" She was breathing hard when she finished, and I could see she was close to losing the control she had on those tears she was fighting back.

I cupped her face with both my hands, which only caused her to sniffle and her bottom lip to slightly jut out.

"Just because I can't text you or call you doesn't mean I'm not keeping track of you, making sure you're safe. There is no limit to what I will do when it comes to you. I just need you to trust me, Shakespeare. Wait on me. And don't go out with another man," I told her, then used my thumb to catch the tear that slid down her cheek.

"I don't understand," she whispered. "I miss you. I miss texting you. Our back-and-forth. If I'd known sex was going to end that, I don't think—" Her voice broke, and another tear slipped out. "I don't think I would have done it."

Fuck. This was ripping my chest wide open. Damn them all for this! She'd done nothing, and she was suffering. I couldn't let their fucking commands continue to hurt her.

The doors opened, and I moved a hand to her back and nodded my head toward the hall before I led her out. Turning right, we went to the end of the long hallway to the last door that belonged to the suite I'd managed to secure us.

There were probably some rooms in hotels nearby that were more affordable and easier to get, but they weren't in this hotel, and I hadn't wanted to take her out into the insanity to fight through the crowds to get to another one. And they didn't have the ball-drop view that this one had. I wanted her to have that. I wanted to be with her when it fell, ringing in the new year.

Two hundred grand in cash and thirty grand worth of Carver's Bootleg Whiskey had been the cost. I hadn't even flinched.

When we reached the door, I used the key card, then pushed it open for her to go inside. Stepping in behind her, I saw the white twinkling lights from the Christmas tree I'd ordered to be set up in here. She hadn't put one up in her apartment this year, and from all our text over the years, I knew that putting up a tree was normally a big deal for her. She'd make cookies and play Christmas movies, and often, Jellie would take the train over from Boston to join her.

There hadn't been one cheerful, over-the-top decoration that she'd talked about in the past anywhere in sight. That was my fault too. I'd taken her holiday joy from her, and fuck if I wasn't going to make up for it the best I could.

"Th-there's a tree," she said with a touch of awe in her voice.

"And the chocolate-covered strawberries and cupcakes are both gluten-free," I said, walking up behind her as she stood, taking in the scene.

Nancy, the head at the concierge desk, hadn't let me down. But then I'd handed her three grand, rolled up and secured with a rubber band, to get this done quickly.

She shook her head, and her shoulders drooped when she wrapped her arms around herself in a dejected way. "I don't understand you, Ransom." Her words were barely above a whisper.

Yeah, she did. What she didn't understand were the reasons behind my actions. That was the fucking family controlling me.

"I handled some things wrong. I was rash, and because of that, I've had orders placed on me," I told her.

I wasn't supposed to tell her anything, but I no longer gave a shit. They were making me hurt her over and over, and I couldn't do that anymore. I wanted my girl smiling, happy. I wanted her to light up at the sight of me, the way my chest soared when I saw her. I didn't like the tears. I fucking hated the tears. They were worse than any torture the family might choose to punish me with.

She turned, and her head tilted back as she stared up at me. "What orders?" she asked, concern taking the place of pain.

Closing the space between us, I slid a hand over her hip and rested it there. Needing to touch her to ease some of the savagery that had taken over me since I'd gotten the call from Wayne.

"Family orders, Shakespeare. Ones handed down from the boss. The man who holds the power to decide if I live or die. That is the only reason I obeyed. But now," I said with a shake of my head, "I don't care about that. Not if this is hurting you so much that you went out with another man. Fuck, Shakespeare, I can't even look at other women and feel anything. I don't want them. I don't acknowledge them. Just you. It's just you."

The softening of her expression didn't ease the look in her eyes. Instead, they appeared more alarmed than anything else. "Live or die?" she asked.

I nodded and reached up to brush the pad of my thumb over her bottom lip. "It's the life. You obey the boss."

"No, wait." She stepped away from my touch, shaking her head. "Are you telling me that your being here is going to get you ... get you killed?" The franticness in her tone was cute.

"I hope not," I replied. "Doesn't matter. I'm here, and it's the only place I want to be."

She held up a hand, her eyes wide as she shook her head. "Noooo, it does matter. You can't just ... you can't d-die. I

139

can't—I don't—" She let out a breath and blinked as another tear rolled down her face. "I can't live in a world you're not in, Ransom. If that means you can't be with me or even contact me, then go. Please, if you feel anything for me, you will go," she said, pointing to the door.

I probably should have softened that truth up for her. She wasn't ready to hear all that my life entailed yet. It would take time to slowly ease her into it. If I had that time. I fucking hope I did. I wanted a lifetime with this woman.

"That was worst case," I told her. "I doubt that I'll meet my end for tonight. I didn't tell you that to upset you, Shakespeare. I told you so you'd understand that my silence doesn't mean what you think. And the necklace," I smirked with a shake of my head. "You wrote the damn book, baby. How did you not understand the meaning behind it?"

She stilled, and I could see her mind working. As it began to sink in—what that necklace had meant—the slight O of her lips made me want to grab her and slam my mouth down on hers. But fucking her like an animal against the nearest hard surface wasn't what she needed … yet.

"You … did you read all my books?" she asked hesitantly.

I nodded. "I couldn't hear your voice, so I read your words. Several times, in fact."

She blew out a breath as her eyes began to fill up with tears. "Oh," she whispered. "Oh."

I waited for her to say more and had to literally grit my teeth as I fought the urge to go take her in my arms.

"So, the books," she said as her eyes scanned my face.

I nodded. "Yeah."

Lifting both hands, she wiped at her cheeks as a small laugh bubbled out of her. "It was you. I thought—I didn't know what to think. Those are … they're rare. I know because I did research on them when writing the book."

I nodded. They were fucking rare and not cheap to secure. But I loved seeing them on the camera when I checked her apartment. Sitting there on her shelf, displayed. She was proud of them.

Her hand went to her bare neck, where the necklace I had given her would have looked stunning. But I assumed it was still shoved in the back of that drawer she'd put it in.

"The necklace, it was … it was because …" Her brows drew together as she studied me.

"Because it was his promise of forever, a symbol of his love, and he didn't want her wearing that on her finger. He wanted it near her heart to remind her she owned his," I finished for her. The shit was that romantic bullshit women loved and what had made her millions. But I liked the idea of it.

"Forever?" she asked, hope finally shining in her pretty eyes.

I nodded. However long that might be for me. But I didn't say that. It would put a damper on things, and I wanted her happy tonight. I had making up to do.

When she said nothing more but wiped at more tears, I closed the space she'd put between us.

She had to tilt her head back further to look at me when I pulled her against me.

"You don't believe in forever. You've told me a million times that men get tired of one, uh …"

"Cunt," I provided, biting back a grin.

She nodded. "Yes, that. They get bored and want someone new. They like variety. No commitment."

I'd said a lot of shit that I believed.

"Yeah, Shakespeare, I did. But you went and fucking stole my soul, baby. Changed the rules. Now, all I can see or want is you."

141

The corners of her mouth began to curl up in a smile. God, I loved that smile. I'd seen little of it lately. I'd made a man disappear because he had some claim on her. My possessiveness had kicked in first. It took my heart a moment to catch up.

I touched the spot where the eight carat sapphire would rest if she had worn the necklace. "After tonight, when we fuck, I want you naked with my promise of forever right here."

She bit her bottom lip nervously. "I almost wore it tonight, but, well, it's expensive. I was scared of wearing it on the subway. If I wear it out in public, I might get mugged."

Grinning, I bent my head and pressed a kiss to the corner of her mouth, unable to hold back any longer. "I have insurance on it," I assured her.

"But," she breathed, turning her head to give me better access, "I don't want to ever lose it."

"You won't."

She let out a small, breathy laugh as I nipped at her bottom lip with my teeth. "This is New York City. Mugging is a thing."

I tugged her closer and brushed my lips against the soft spot just below her ear. "Baby, if someone is stupid enough to take it off you, I'll hunt them down, retrieve it, and kill them."

Her body stiffened, and she pulled back so she could see my face. There was a frown between her brows. "Don't say that. You're not killing anyone."

Eh, well, that was one thing I couldn't promise her. I didn't get a choice in that matter. But right now, we were going to let that fact go.

"Shakespeare," I said instead.

"Yes?"

"I love you."

TWENTY

NOA

Not three words I'd anticipated hearing Ransom Carver say. Sure, he'd said he wanted forever, but even then, I hadn't thought he'd say that he loved me. I was wired to believe he didn't fall in love. He fucked. He enjoyed variety. Things he had told me so many times over the years that it was just who he was in my head. This version of him was foreign yet not. There was a familiarity to it.

"You love me," I said softly as that sank in.

He nodded, grinning at me, as if my reaction was amusing. I probably looked stunned.

"You … that … this …" I stopped my stammering because finding the right words seemed important, but my head was reeling. As was my heart.

"Yes?" he replied as he watched me struggle to speak.

"I'm sorry. I just wasn't expecting you to ever say that to me," I said.

He held my chin between his thumb and forefinger. "Was it that shocking, Shakespeare? I'd just told you I wanted forever."

I blinked. He was serious about this.

"A man doesn't do the insane shit I've done because of you for a woman who doesn't own him. You *own* me. You have for a while. It just took me some time to figure it out."

Own him? Me?

"I feel like I've stepped into my own book," I whispered.

He leaned down closer to me and winked. "How am I doing?"

"What?" I asked, confused.

"I know it's not a luxurious overwater bungalow in the Maldives, but it's the best I could do under the circumstances."

Bungalow in the Maldives. That was where Draven, the hero in my first three books, had taken Hannah, the heroine, when he told her he loved her, then put the necklace around her neck. Ransom really had read all my books. That hadn't been a joke.

"Are you telling me you're trying to act like Draven?" I asked him.

He smirked. "I don't have to try hard. The man looks like me, talks like me—eh, the majority of the time—and he has a thing for women in libraries. Pretty fucking similar already."

I pressed my lips together to stifle my laugh, but it didn't do much good. The bubble of laughter found its way past them anyway. I felt my cheeks warm. He had pieced all that together. My little fantasy that I'd written of another life. One where the gorgeous, sexy bad boy fell for the librarian.

His hand cupped my cheek. "Don't go blushing now," he teased. "I know all about your dirty fantasies with me. And I intend to play every one of them out. Then we can work on giving you some new inspiration."

I licked my lips as my heart fluttered in my chest while his eyes drifted over my face.

"We can move on to the next chapter as soon as you finish your lines," he said, stopping his gaze when it locked with mine.

"What lines?" I asked.

He leaned down and pressed a kiss to my cheek as one of his hands slid around to cup, then squeeze my butt. "The part where you tell me you love me, Shakespeare."

A smile slid across my face as he began to inch the silky fabric of my dress up while peppering small kisses along my jawline.

"I didn't know it was necessary," I said breathlessly, arching my neck for him to continue on. "You read the books after all."

He made a small growling noise. "Not the same. I need to hear you say it." His fingers dug into the plump flesh of my bottom, causing me to yelp.

"'Draven wasn't that rough," I said.

"Not wanting to emulate him, Shakespeare. Just perfect him. He needed more edge," Ransom said, then sank his teeth into the curve of my neck.

I wasn't sure there was a time I hadn't loved him. Even in my youth, he'd made my pulse race and stirred something inside me that no one else ever had. Perhaps our souls had known it before we did. That they belonged together. We had just needed to grow up, become the people we were today.

"I love you," I said, causing him to still.

His head lifted, and his golden eyes met mine.

We stood there like that for several moments. Silence surrounding us. The outside noise faded away.

"I know, but, fuck, I like hearing you say it," he finally said. Then his eyes darkened, and he lifted his chin slightly in the direction of the sitting area behind me. "Go grab the back of the sofa and stick out your juicy ass for me."

This version of Ransom I was familiar with. Willing to do anything the man asked of me, I turned and went over to it and obeyed.

"Did he touch what's mine?" he asked. His tone was hoarse and edged with something dangerous.

I shook my head. "No, I wasn't with him. That's one of Jellie's brothers. He was just here so I wouldn't be a third wheel. Jellie had asked him to come. Not me."

Shivering as he pulled up my dress until it was bunched at my waist, I waited for him to say more.

"If it wasn't a date, why are you dressed like a fucking wet dream?" he asked, running his hand between my legs.

"Oh!" I moaned as his fingers slid beneath the thin strap of fabric that ran between my butt cheeks and did little to cover the rest of me as well.

"Talk, baby," he urged, "or this stops, and I spank your ass."

"I'm not—I mean, this is a dress I owned, all I had that looked festive," I explained.

"Hmm." He stepped closer and slid a finger inside me. "I didn't like the way he looked at you." His lips brushed my temple, and my knees wobbled as he continued to slowly explore the wetness pooling between my legs. "I didn't like the familiarity. He was too comfortable getting close to you."

I shook my head. "He-he's like my family."

"You sure he feels that way?" His voice took on an edge.

"Yes," I panted, closing my eyes and holding on to the sofa.

"Whose pussy is this?" he asked huskily in my ear, and I shivered.

"Yours."

"Mmm, that's right. Mine." The last word was a pleased rumble in his chest. "I need to fuck you."

"Yes," I pleaded, wanting that very much.

146

"I was going to be sweet and romantic and shit, but, fuuuuck, your naked ass and soaked cunt have my cock already leaking."

Oh God. I'd missed this. His dirty mouth. The sound of his voice.

"Please," I begged, wiggling my bottom against him.

He growled a curse, and his hand was gone. I glanced back over my shoulder to see him unzipping his jeans and shoving them down until his cock jutted out—thick, hard, and swollen at the tip. The glistening of his pre-cum made me moan again.

"Can't wait," he snarled as he jerked the silk panties aside and looked down at me. "Spread those pretty thighs."

Opening them more, I leaned over further so that I was on full display.

"Dayum, baby," he muttered, then slapped down hard on my left butt cheek, making me squeal. "That's for letting another man take you anywhere. Especially dressed like this."

I didn't respond but watched, holding my breath, as he palmed his erection, then stepped closer to run it along my slick folds. A deep hum came from him before he lined the tip up with my entrance, then slammed into me with one hard thrust.

"Fuck yes!" he shouted as I cried out from the pleasure and the pain. "My fucking pussy!"

Yes. It was his. I was his. All of it was his. Right now, I would promise him anything. If the package came with him, then I'd take it.

He grabbed my hair and wrapped it around his fist, pulling my head back so that my back was arched. "When I'm not worrying about you, missing you, I'm thinking about fucking you. How this tight little cunt feels, sucking my cock

147

so hungrily," he said in a savage voice. "You take my dick like such a good girl."

I would take it in any position, but I did miss the way his piercing hit my clit when I rode him or he was on top. The desperate dirtiness of having him spank me and take me from behind with my panties still on had its own set of pleasures though. Even without his piercing's added effect. I liked the depravity and animalistic urgency of being fucked like this.

"Oh, oh." I was already so close.

Turning my head, I realized you could see our reflection in the picture window that overlooked Times Square. His jawline stood out as his focus was on my butt as it slapped against him. He was beautiful all the time, but like this, he was breathtaking. Every muscle in his body was flexed, and his mouth was slightly open.

"Are you watching us?" he asked, and my eyes shot up to see he'd cut his in the same direction. "You see how pretty that ass is, bouncing off me?"

No. I saw how he looked like Adonis, pumping into me like a man who couldn't get enough.

"I'm gonna come," I wailed as it hit me. My body shook, and my knees started to give out as the onslaught of blissful release shot through me.

"FUCK!" he yelled as his body jerked behind me.

The swell of his cock stretched me just before his release pulsed inside me, hot and thick. Slowing his hips, he continued to penetrate me as deeply as before but easier.

I dropped my head to the back of the sofa I had been holding on to and tried to catch my breath.

"Stay like that," he said gruffly and eased out of me.

I felt his hands slide over my bottom, then pull it apart.

Lifting my head, I glanced over my shoulder to see what he was doing. Because as incredible as that had been, I was not open for business in the other hole.

There was a predatory gleam in his eyes as he stared between my legs. "Squeeze your cunt muscles for me," he instructed.

I realized then he wasn't checking out my ass, but he was watching his semen as it leaked from me. I bit my bottom lip as I smiled and did as he'd requested. I could feel it trickle out onto my inner thighs.

"Mmm," he murmured. He said nothing more, but watched with fascination.

When he finally lifted his eyes to mine, he smirked. "The only thing hotter than the sight of your wet pink pussy is seeing my cum oozing out of it."

I laughed, then buried my face in my hands. When he started the dirty talk and we weren't worked up, having sex or about to, I was shy about it.

He chuckled. "Come here." His hand wrapped around my arm, and he helped me stand back up. "Are your cheeks pink from blushing or flushed from fucking?" he asked, curling me into his arms.

"Both," I replied against his chest.

"My naughty writer is blushing over my obsession with seeing her pussy leaking my cum. That's cute."

I laughed. He was right, of course. I'd written more explicit things than what we'd just done.

"We have thirty minutes before the ball drops," he said, pressing his lips against my temple. "Let's open the champagne and have some of the treats. I'll wait until after the fireworks before I get you naked."

"Can we see the ball drop from here?" I asked, lifting my head to look back at the window.

149

I hadn't paid close enough attention when we came inside. Most of the curtains had been pulled together. The part that was open in the middle didn't show much more than the lights from outside.

"It's our first New Year's Eve together. Hell yeah, you can see the ball drop from here. Would Draven have gotten Hannah a fucking hotel room that didn't overlook Times Square?"

I grinned and looked back up at him. "No," I replied.

"That fucker ain't gonna outdo me."

TWENTY-ONE
NOA

We were curled up on the sofa—where Ransom had moved it so that it was not only beside the Christmas tree, but in direct view of the New Year's Eve ball—and nothing else mattered. Not right now. Maybe it would later, but I wanted to memorize every detail of this moment. Keep it close. The warmth, the joy, the feeling of peace. As if I were finally home. Not my apartment. That was just where I lived. Home was a place I'd been searching for all my life. Ransom Carver's arms had been that magical location all along.

"Might want to deal with this," Ransom said as he leaned forward to take my phone I'd left on the table, which he'd also pulled closer so that we had easy access to the champagne and treats. "Keeps lighting up."

I looked down at my cell to see Jellie's name and winced. Shit! I had forgotten all about her and the VIP party I had vanished from without a word.

Sliding my hand over the screen to answer, I glanced up at Ransom.

"Hey, I am so sorry. My phone was on silent," I said to her before she could say anything.

"OH-MY-GOD, Noa! Where are you? I've called at least twenty times!"

She was sober now. I guessed my *missing person* thing had done that to her.

"I'm sorry," I repeated, feeling guilty. "I …" I paused as I stared at Ransom questioningly.

What did I tell her? She knew little about him. Did he want anyone to know he was here?

He nodded his head, as if for me to continue.

Do I tell her I'm with you? I mouthed silently.

He nodded again. "Make sure her brother knows that too."

The territorial gleam in his eyes as he said it would have made me laugh if I wasn't feeling like an asshole for running off and not thinking to tell her.

"Um, see, I went to the restroom, and I ran into an old friend," I started.

Ransom began shaking his head, so I stopped and frowned. What was it he wanted me to say?

He held out his hand for the phone. When I didn't hand it to him, he cocked an eyebrow.

"Noa!" Jellie said, still sounding panicked. "I know you went to the restroom. Birch was there. But where did you go? He even went into the women's restroom and searched it!"

I saw Ransom's jaw tic, and I knew he could hear her. He didn't seem happy about Birch's concern. Since I had no clue what I should say, I reluctantly handed him my phone.

"Jellie." His thick drawl said her name in a way that made me smile despite the situation. "This is Ransom Carver. I believe you know me as an old friend of Noa's from Madison. I met a friend of yours while wearing a bath towel at Noa's apartment."

She was going to die. I bit my bottom lip while trying to hear what she said, but I couldn't make it out.

"Yes," he replied. "I wanted Noa to myself tonight. I hope that's okay. She's safely at the hotel in a suite I booked for the two of us, overlooking Times Square. You can enjoy your evening. I'll take care of her."

He paused, and I could hear her talking, but still, I could only make out a few words.

"With my life," he replied. "And, Jellie, no more setups. Noa isn't available. She's mine."

He held out the phone to me then without waiting on her response to that.

Oh good Lord, she was going to flip out about this. How would I ever get off the phone with her?

"Hey," I said, not sure what else to say.

"Noa Raines, what in the actual hell?! That is tattoo guy! Muscled, badass tattoo guy! You have been lying to me! He came to get you. He called you his!" She was shouting, but there was an excitement to her tone.

"It's been complicated." That wasn't going to calm her down, but I didn't have the time to waste talking about this right now.

"How did he even get into the party? Did he call you and you went out to meet him? And he got a room here? That's not possible."

She was prattling on with one question after another. If I didn't stop her, this would go on all night.

"Jellie, I will talk to you about this tomorrow. It's New Year's Eve. I want to ... enjoy the rest of it with Ransom."

"You're happy then? Is he why you've been upset?"

I should have known that she hadn't bought my fake attempt at appearing normal.

"Yes. But we've worked things out."

153

There was a pause.

"Okay. But tomorrow, you have to give me every detail. All of it."

I knew I couldn't do that, but I smiled. "I will."

"Whew. I have so many questions right now. Just know that the fact that I am holding them all in is due to my love for you," she told me, sounding exasperated.

"Thank you."

"Happy New Year, Noa."

"Happy New Year," I replied before ending the call.

Ransom took my phone and placed it on the table, then picked up the champagne flute he'd poured me earlier and handed it to me.

"I won't actually tell her everything," I assured him.

His gaze met mine. "I know. But I don't mind if you want to share just how hard I make you come. I'd like the brother to be made aware that I've already claimed this pussy. He needs to go sniffing elsewhere."

I had to cover my mouth to keep from spitting the champagne I'd just taken a sip of. My eyes watered as some went up my nose and burned. He smirked as he watched me.

"Might as well have her spread the word to the other brother, too, in case he has any intentions of trying to move in on what belongs to me."

"I told you they were like my brothers."

He shook his head. "No, baby. No straight man is going to think of a woman who looks like you as his sister if they aren't related," he told me as he wrapped a strand of my hair around his finger. "But damn if I don't love how fucking naive you are. It's cute."

I narrowed my eyes. "I am not naive."

"Yeah, Shakespeare, you are. Trusting, kind, thoughtful, witty, smart, adorable, sexy as hell, and incredibly naive." He reached over with his other hand and pinched my chin, tilting my head back further. "You're fucking precious."

Okay, so maybe I could live with being called naive. My stomach fluttered, and every cell in my body tingled. Oh, what my sixteen-year-old self would have thought if she'd known one day that Ransom Carver would call her all of those things. I smiled, thinking about her, the girl I had once been. She was so lost and broken, but she'd been a fighter.

If only I could go back and tell her how proud I was of her and what all she would overcome.

"All I have is tonight," he said huskily. "I'll have to go handle things in the morning. You might not hear from me for a while. But you will be all I think about. I'll watch over you. I'll know where you are and if you need me. But I can't be with you. Not right now. I just need you to trust me."

I swallowed as my throat began to tighten. What was it he had to do? After all this, I had thought he'd be coming back to my apartment and staying for a couple of days.

"Your number was disconnected," I told him.

He'd not explained that. Actually, there was a lot he hadn't explained, but I was going to leave it for tomorrow. I had wanted tonight to be magical. But if he wasn't going to be here …

"I know. That wasn't my doing. I have another. I can't give it to you because I don't know if your calls are being traced."

"My calls?" I asked, confused.

He nodded, then let out a heavy sigh. "Yeah. Shit I can't tell you, Shakespeare, and I'm sorry. When it's over, I will explain. But for now, trust me."

I swallowed hard, not wanting to ask the next question, but needing to know at the same time.

"When you said your being here was going to get you killed …" The last word got stuck in my throat.

He shook his head. "I'll be fine." Then he leaned down and pressed a kiss to my lips. Gentle, the briefest brush. "I have too much to live for, Shakespeare. We have that forever I promised you'd get."

TWENTY-TWO
RANSOM

This was peace. The silence. Noa curled up against my chest, asleep, my fingers slipping through her silky locks as I watched her. I much preferred this version of observing her while she slept. I could hold her, touch her, and even feel her heart beating, see the pulse in her neck, watch her slow, even breathing up close. I didn't want to ever fucking leave.

But that wasn't my reality. If I wanted this—and I did, more than my next breath—then I had to go. I wanted her safe and away from the dangers of my life, but I also needed her so goddamn much. It wasn't fair, but had my life ever been fair? I'd not been born into a family where I got to make my own decisions. I didn't have the freedom to decide I wanted to move off and do something different.

Truth was, I'd never resented it until now. Until I was told I couldn't have the one thing on this earth I was willing to die to have. Her. Noa. My Shakespeare. The girl who had charmed me with her wit and brain alone when she was only sixteen. Even back then, when shit got dark, I had found myself thinking of her last witty comment, and I'd text her. Needing to be distracted. To smile.

If I were any other man, I wouldn't have heard it. The smallest click. Most would have assumed it was another guest going into the room nearby. But I wasn't most. I knew exactly what it was, but the who I wasn't certain of.

Easing my arm out from under Noa, I slipped from the bed, grabbing my jeans without bothering to find my briefs, and jerked them on silently. I reached under the mattress, where I'd hidden my .22, just as the light from the hallway spilled ever so briefly into the entryway.

Flattening myself against the wall, I eased closer to the corner, where whoever had the disengage tool on hand to unlock the bolt to a hotel room door was just as fucking silent as me. This was family. It had to be. They'd found me. I probably had a goddamn tracker on me and didn't realize it.

I was fucking pissed. Linc could have stayed out there and called me. I'd have come out. They didn't have to break into the room where Noa slept. Damn him and his commands. This wasn't her fault, and they had no right getting so damn close to her. If she woke up, she'd be terrified. It was best I faced them and left quietly. Although I didn't even have on my boots.

When no one appeared, I cocked my piece and stepped into the line of sight. A cold dread iced my veins. It wasn't Bane or Oz.

"Well, happy New Year to you too, Carver."

The eerily languid tone didn't fool me. I knew who it was, even in the darkness. He didn't even have his gun pulled. Instead, he stood, leaning against the wall with an unlit cigarette in his mouth and his arms crossed over his chest, as if he had been waiting for me. Inside the family, there was only one crazier son of a bitch than the one staring at me now. And honestly, I thought I'd have preferred the other one. Because the real psychopath wasn't Blaise Hughes's best friend.

This one was.

Which meant he wasn't here on Linc's orders. The boss had sent him.

"Gage," I replied.

"Real nice room you got. Bet that view was something," Gage Presley said as he pulled out a lighter from his pocket and flicked it, illuminating his face. That was his biggest weapon. His looks. He was even fucking prettier than Oz, but unlike Oz, the man had no soul.

And this was who Blaise had sent to get me. My future had just been shortened.

"Where are we going?" I asked, already knowing the answer.

He shoved off from the wall and inhaled. "Ah, back where the sun is shining and it's a brisk sixty-five degrees."

Ocala. To the Hugheses' property. The billion-dollar horse racing ranch that also housed the most dangerous and powerful man in the South.

I glanced back across the large suite at the bed one last time to see Noa sleeping peacefully. The chances that this would be the last time I saw her were pretty damn high. I might not even see another sunset. But if this was it, then at least she knew how I felt. I'd said the words. I'd told her I loved her. I'd held her, fucked her, worshipped her, kissed her several times tonight. If she was safe, then I had my peace.

"Okay," I replied, lowering my gun. "Let me grab my shirt and boots," I told him.

He took the cigarette from his lips. "Not even gonna make this fun?" he asked with a smirk.

159

He fucking knew I wasn't going to refuse to leave with him. Just like Blaise had known it when he sent him to get me.

"We leave, she's unharmed—that's all I care about," I replied. Although leaving her here without an explanation or goodbye was fucking painful.

He cocked a brow. "All right, get your boots, lover boy, and let's go."

My gaze went back to her, and the only thing keeping me from going over there and looking at her face one more time was the psycho in the room. Walking over, I picked up my discarded shirt, socks, and boots, then slid my wallet back into my pocket, along with both cell phones. The one I thought I had taken the only tracker out of but apparently they'd had another one on me too and the one no one knew about.

Starting to turn and head toward the door, I saw the hotel stationery on the entry desk with a pen. I paused and looked from it to Gage. "Just let me write her a goodbye."

He inhaled deeply, then let it out through his nose as he stared at me. "Tell me something," he said, looking relaxed and at ease. "Would you burn down a house for her? Not give a fuck who was in it?"

I glanced at her again. "I'd burn down a goddamn county." And I wished I'd burned down Ocala, but it was too late now.

His chuckle was low with an unhinged sound to it that reminded me of just who I was talking to. "Make it quick," he said, then took another pull from the cigarette and leaned his shoulder against the wall, watching me.

Picking up the pen, I knew he'd read whatever I wrote. He could see it from where he stood. I couldn't tell her why or where I was headed. But if these were my last words to her, I wanted them to count.

FOREVER HAS NO TIME FRAME. YOU OWN MY SOUL IN THIS LIFE
AND THE ONES TO COME.

—RANSOM

When I laid the pen down, breathing became hard.
Inhaling only made the agony in my chest more unbearable.

"Well, aren't you a fucking poet?" Gage said with
amusement.

And aren't you a fucking psychopath?

TWENTY-THREE

RANSOM

Opening my one good eye, I winced from the pounding in my head. It took me a moment to remember what had happened, but it came back the moment I took in my surroundings. I was underground, except not in Madison. I was in Ocala. The first underground facilities of the family. The caves built by Jediah Hughes, the founder of the Southern Mafia, and Charles Shephard, his best friend, almost one hundred twenty years ago.

Fucking Gage had brought me down here, tied me up, and then slammed his fist into my temple. I didn't know how long ago that had been, but from the numbness in my extended arms, I was guessing at least four hours. Maybe five. I scanned the room to find no one. They'd left me alone down here. I had that to be grateful for.

I'd imagined my death to be a swift thing. A bullet between the eyes. That was Blaise's typical way of taking out someone he didn't feel he needed to torture for information first or retaliation. I'd disobeyed an order. That might mean death, but torture? It was a little extreme.

My thoughts drifted to the one place that I always escaped to when shit was bad. Noa. Closing my good eye that hadn't been affected by the hit I'd taken from Gage, I let her smile and the sound of her laugh replay in my memory. Last night had been perfect, and if I had known this would be the outcome, I'd still have fucking done it. Every second I'd take with me to the grave. Hopefully, the hell thing was bullshit. I was banking on the reincarnation theory. That my soul would have another life, not end up burning in eternal damnation—or whatever it was that the Christians put on those billboards.

The echo of footsteps had me snapping my eye open again, and I watched the door, waiting to see who was coming for me. I knew the shit that was done down here. Mentally preparing myself for it was easier than I would have thought. If they were going to make me live without Noa in this life, then what the fuck was it worth? They'd already done their worst, taking her from me.

The man who filled the doorway wasn't Blaise. He was bigger, wider shoulders, arms the size of my fucking thighs and bulging with cut, defined muscles. That bastard had to be on steroids. No one was that damn built naturally. Not even if he lived in the gym.

Regardless of his intimidating appearance, it was a relief. He was the lesser of the evils. Huck Kingston wasn't known for being a psycho, nor was he the boss. I doubted Blaise would send him to do the dirty work of taking me out.

"Your arms numb yet?" he asked as he entered the room.

"Yeah," I replied hoarsely from my dry throat. At least if I was dehydrated, I wouldn't have to piss.

He crossed his arms over his massive chest while holding a bottle of water in one hand and sighed heavily. "All this for a woman." He shook his head. "Figures."

He was happily married, last time I'd checked. But then so was Blaise. Didn't seem to matter to him that I was being told I couldn't be with the woman I loved. Yet they all got to have their women. Protect them. Keep them in their beds. Fuckers.

"You want some water? Been down here about six hours," he said.

I shook my head.

"You're gonna dehydrate."

"Does that really fucking matter?" I asked. Seriously. I wasn't walking out of here alive. Who cared about being hydrated?

He shrugged. "Guess not."

Dropping his hands, he walked over to the workbench, where they kept several of their tools meant to get people to talk, a pack of Marlboros, a lighter, and a half-empty bottle of whiskey. He placed the bottle of water there as well. My eyes followed him as I waited for him to say more. Do something. Give me a goddamn timeline on when I would be taking my last breath.

"Boss is a little tied up. Linc arrived an hour ago," he said, glancing back at me as he picked up a knife and hung it on a nail above the table. "More accurately, it was more like the cavalry. Hale, Bane, Luther," he said, then reached down to pull out a stool and take a seat.

My dad was here. I hadn't expected that. I actually hadn't expected Linc to come, much less the rest of them. The first stirrings of hope that this might not be my end began, but I said nothing. I didn't want to show any weakness. I was already tied up with a swollen, shut eye.

"They're all in Blaise's office," he informed me. "Talking things through."

What things? There'd better be no deals made in exchange for my life. Noa remained untouched and unscathed. Her life went on the way it always had, and she was none the wiser to this side of my world. That was something I'd die to protect.

"Not much to talk through," I said. "I disobeyed an order. Pretty cut and dry."

Huck's eyes narrowed. "Are you wanting to die, Carver?"

No. But I wanted Noa. And if I couldn't have her, life wouldn't be tolerable.

"I want Noa safe. I want her left out of this," I said through clenched teeth.

He crossed his tattooed arms over his chest again. "If you're six feet under, you can't make sure that happens. Did Gage hit you too hard? Not thinking clearly."

Unlike Gage, Huck didn't taunt. He was direct and businesslike. Both men worked directly under Blaise Hughes. They were in that position for a couple of reasons. However, Huck's reasons weren't the same as Gage's.

While Gage hadn't been born into the family and had been accepted in because he was Blaise Hughes's best friend, Huck was a descendant of one of Jediah's closest childhood friends, Mars Kingston. Jediah brought him into the family in the early 1920s. Every son after him had worked directly with the current Hughes boss. He had grown up with the future boss, trained with him, killed with him.

"You're giving up too soon, Carver," he said with a shake of his head. "You fucked up. But Blaise isn't one to act without thought. He's reasonable."

A hard laugh escaped me before I could stop it. There was nothing reasonable about the Southern Mafia boss.

Huck raised his brows. "You don't think so?"

"He put a bullet in his stepsister," I said, pointing out just how heartless the man was.

Huck nodded. "He did. But he'd let her live after she took Maddy and handed her to strangers."

Yeah, I knew the story, and that didn't make him reasonable. "Those strangers were working for Maddy's father. The one she didn't know she had." I said with a trace of sarcasm in my tone.

Maddy, Blaise's wife, had never been in danger when she was handed over to the members of the Judgment MC.

"Point made," he agreed. "But let me ask you this. What if a female took Noa, broke her arm, terrorized her? What would you do?"

"I'd kill her."

His almost smile was smug. "Exactly. And Levi would have done it if Blaise hadn't. Blaise did what had to be done for the family. Gina wasn't going to stop. She was obsessed with Levi, and as long as she was alive, Aspen wasn't safe."

Aspen was Levi's wife. I hadn't realized Gina, Blaise Hughes former step-sister, had broken Aspen's arm and terrorized her. I just knew she'd taken her from where she worked. Linc hadn't given us any real details, but he had to have known. Levi was his son.

Huck stretched and stood back up. "Blaise is ruthless. He protects his name and power. But," he said, leveling me with his gaze, "part of that power is ruling with a fair hand inside the family. You still have a chance of walking out of here."

I didn't respond. I was currently strung up and in the caves. And if I couldn't have Noa, then I wasn't sure leaving was worth it.

Huck picked up the bottle of water he'd placed on the table and opened it, then walked over to me. "Drink the damn water, Carver."

I glared at him, then opened my mouth, and he poured some inside. At least it would be easier to swallow now that it didn't feel as if I'd been eating cotton.

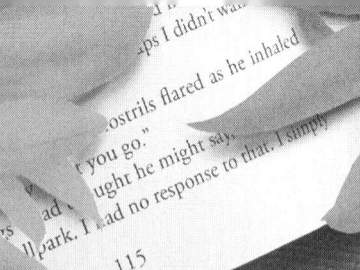

TWENTY-FOUR
NOA

The paper trembled in my hand as I stood, staring down at it. Rereading the words over and over. Each time more difficult than the time before.

When I'd awoken alone, I'd thought for a moment that Ransom had stepped out to get something. I couldn't believe he'd just left me. He'd promised Jellie he would get me home—not that I needed him to get home, but still. He hadn't said he was leaving.

His underwear—the black boxer briefs—was still tossed on the floor by the sofa, where he'd taken them off last night. He wouldn't have left without wearing his underwear.

I'd gotten up and used the supplies in the bathroom that the hotel had left out to brush my teeth with some mouth-wash and a cotton swab, then swooshed the rest around in my mouth. I even washed my face and used the restroom. When thirty minutes passed, I walked to stare out the window at the street below, wondering if he'd gone to pick up something special for breakfast and gotten caught up in the still-crowded streets.

I turned around to see if there was a bottle of water in the refrigerator, and it was then that I noticed the pad of paper on the desk had writing on it. My heart sank. I knew without looking that he hadn't stepped out.

He'd left me. Again.

FOREVER HAS NO TIME FRAME. YOU OWN MY SOUL IN THIS LIFE AND THE ONES TO COME.

—RANSOM

What did this mean? The more I read it, the more it sounded as if … as if … he hadn't gone because he wanted to.

His underwear had been left behind. My imagination, being elaborate, had many different scenarios running through my mind, and each one seemed to be more unthinkable than the next.

I had no way to contact him. No number. Nothing.

Fear crawled up my spine slowly, and my stomach knotted so tightly that I felt nauseated.

Oh God. What if something bad had happened to him? He'd rushed out without his boxers. They were in plain sight. He hadn't overlooked them. Was he on the run?

I started to put the note down, but I couldn't let go of it. He'd touched it. Written this to me. Holding it felt like I had some connection to him. Right now, this was all I had. Gently, I folded it and held it in my hand.

I was wearing the hotel robe and needed to get dressed. I also had to think. There had to be a way to contact him. Find him.

The heavy foreboding that was seeping through me was a monster I couldn't control.

What if I was overreacting? This could have just been reassurance that he'd be back. His reminder to wait for me.

But what if I wasn't?

What if he needed help and I did nothing? I couldn't lose him. I wouldn't survive it.

I had to go to Madison. I knew where his house was. That was the only option I had. I could go, and ... and ... what? Go to his security gate and ask to see him? That wouldn't get him in any trouble. I wouldn't be the first female to come looking for him. Or I could go to the distillery. That was a better idea.

He had said to trust him. But he'd also said being here might get him killed and the thing about my calls being traced. Questions I had put off until today because I wanted last night to just be about us. Together. Ringing in the new year.

How I wished I'd pressed him for more.

I was going to Madison. If I was overreacting, then it was his fault. He'd told me he was leaving after taking me home, and he'd left his underwear behind. Both of those things were off.

Deep down, it didn't feel like my imagination. There was a warning bell going off in my head that wouldn't shut up. Not to mention, my gut was equally as loud. And until I laid eyes on him, I wouldn't be okay.

It had taken me longer than anticipated to get here. The flight I'd book was delayed three times and then canceled. I had to get another flight with another airline, and it was the last flight out that night. The airport in Jacksonville was empty, except for those getting off our plane, yet it took forever in luggage claim. To make things even more complicated, the rental car counters were all closed, but it was after midnight, so really, I had expected as much. I needed my own car, and it wasn't as if I could pull up to the security gate at Ransom's house in the middle of the night. I had to get a room at the closest hotel and stay the night.

I wasn't sure I'd slept any, but I thought I might have dozed off a time or two. Not that it mattered. I was up, showered, and dressed by six. The Uber I ordered had me at the airport car rentals fifteen minutes before seven, when they opened, and I waited outside the door.

The website to Carver's Bootleg Whiskey said the office hours were ten to five, Monday through Friday. The dates for holiday closures said New Year's Eve and New Year's Day. It was Friday, January 2, and I was hoping they hadn't decided to remain closed for a long weekend. Someone had to be there. At least that was what I was telling myself as I drove the thirty minutes in my rental, thinking of a multitude of scenarios that could play out when I got there.

If the distillery was closed, then I'd go to the house. Press that intercom-button thing on the security gate and ask for Ransom. I didn't like that idea though. If they were tracing my calls, then my showing up might be an issue. Although I hadn't done anything to these people. I still didn't understand why my phone calls were being traced. One more thing he'd not been around to explain to me yesterday morning.

The closer I got, the more anxious I felt.

The turn was up ahead, and the sign on the main road pointing to the entrance sent my anxiety skyrocketing. I had to calm down, or they'd all think I was crazy. The panic attack threatening to take over was hard to fight back. Taking several deep, slow breaths, I focused on that as I came to my turn.

"Please be here," I whispered when I pulled onto the paved drive that led to the distillery.

I'd never been here. I had passed by this place a thousand times in my youth, but not once turned onto this road or drove under the arched sign. It was a big part of Ransom's life, and although I knew a lot about it because of what he'd shared with me over the years, I never actually set foot on the property. I also had no idea what the office building looked like or if it was going to be hard to find.

The bend in the road led me to a large, open parking lot with two buildings. The one on my right was a big industrial-looking structure with oak barrels stacked outside. The one on the right was a log cabin—a rather large log cabin. There were three cars parked out front, and I pulled up beside the truck that I remembered seeing in the garage at Ransom's house. It wasn't his truck, but it had been there. Which meant someone here lived with him. That was a good thing.

My phone started to ring, and Jellie's name lit up the screen. I'd already forwarded one call from her to voicemail yesterday and then texted her that I was writing. But now was not the time to talk. She wanted all the details I wouldn't be giving her about Ransom. Once again, I sent her to voicemail and then put my phone on Do Not Disturb before shoving it in my purse and opening the car door. I would deal with her wrath later.

I barely made it two steps from my car toward the house when the front door swung open, and Than Carver came stalking out. Every photo I'd seen of him smiling and the way Ransom had spoken about him being easygoing and the friendlier out of the two did not fit with his furious expression as he glared at me. I froze, unsure if that rage was centered on me or if I'd just shown up at the wrong time.

"What the fuck are you doing here? Have you not done enough already?" he roared.

ALL TIED UP

I glanced around me to make sure this was directed at me, although I wasn't sure what I had done to cause this reaction from him.

I was alone out here. No one else for him to be talking to.

He pointed to the rental car behind me. "Get in it and get the fuck out of here!"

The door opened again, and Gathe walked out. Was he going to yell at me too? I took one step back but stopped. I couldn't leave. I had to know Ransom was okay.

"Than, dude," he said, grabbing his shoulder, "easy."

Than jerked away from him but kept his murderous expression on me.

"Don't touch me!" he snarled, not looking back at his friend.

Again, the door opened, and a woman stepped out this time. The shocked look on her face made me think perhaps it was just me that brought this reaction out in Than.

"What's going on?" she asked, glancing out at me, then back to Than. Her mass of blonde curls caught the breeze, and she tucked some behind her ear as she walked farther out to where Than was standing.

"She's why they took him," Than said with disgust. "This is all her fucking fault."

The woman looked back at me, then shook her head. "No, it's not her fault. Ransom chose to be with her."

Than turned to look at her. "And he's going to fucking die because of it!" His words held more pain than fury. His voice cracked as he said *die*, and his shoulders rose and fell hard with each breath.

Bile rose in my throat. I was right. It hadn't been my over-active imagination. Ransom hadn't left me of his own free will. But who had taken him?

No longer caring what Than Carver did to me, I walked toward the porch. "Where is he? Who took him?" Terror

173

clawed at my chest, and my gaze swung rapidly from him to the two others up there with him.

If looks could kill, then Than would have just ended my life. He started to take another step in my direction when Gathe grabbed both his shoulders, this time with more force.

"What the fuck, man? She isn't to blame. Ransom wouldn't want you to hurt her," Gathe said as Than began to try and free himself again.

"Does that matter now? He isn't here!" Than roared, and the agony in that sound made my eyes fill with tears.

This was bad. Oh God, where was he? Why had someone taken him?

I shook my head as I gulped for air. "What happened?" I croaked.

"He didn't stay away from you!" Than shouted and broke free, but Gathe darted in front of him and pushed against his chest to keep him back.

"FORGE!" the woman hurried to the door and yelled.

Seconds later, Forge came running outside with his gun in his hand. He glanced from the blonde to the two other guys, now in a full-blown struggle.

"What the fuck?!" he said, shoving his gun back into his holster and reaching to grab hold of Than.

The woman looked at them, then hurried down the steps toward me.

She was stunning, but not young enough to be one of their women. Not that she was old, but she wasn't my age either. I'd guess she was in her early thirties. It didn't matter who she was, if she could tell me what was happening.

My eyes shifted from the men on the porch, then back to her.

"Noa?" she said, as if she was seeking clarification.

I nodded. A tear rolled down my face, and I wiped it away. I'd never felt so helpless in my life.

"I'm Branwen Shephard. My husband ..." She paused. "He's, um ..." She glanced back at the men. "Linc is, uh—"

"He runs the Mississippi branch of the Southern Mafia," I supplied, recognizing his name. Ransom had explained that role already.

She gave me a tight smile. "Yes. Okay, so you know about that," she said.

"Where is Ransom?" I asked, not caring about who her husband was.

The strained expression and glint of fear in her eyes did not make me feel better. Another tear rolled down my face.

"Please," I begged, feeling frantic to know where he was and terrified at the same time that she was going to tell me something that I wouldn't be able to live with.

"He's in Florida," she began.

"Ocala," I whispered, sure that I was about to throw up.

She nodded. "Yes. Linc is there too. And a few others have gone. Ransom's dad."

"Why?" I sobbed, no longer able to keep the emotion back. I was unraveling. Nothing could happen to him.

"He disobeyed a direct order from the boss. Not Linc," she said.

I covered my mouth, and my knees buckled. She became a blur as the flood of tears unleashed.

"Why?" I choked out.

Tears glistened in her eyes, and she pursed her lips, as if she, too, was struggling not to fall apart. "Because he wanted to be with you. He was ordered to stay away."

I shook my head. What had I done? Why would he have been ordered to stay away from me?

"He—" She stopped and inhaled deeply. "He did things for you because he wanted to be with you, and they weren't handled well. It caused some issues. He was ordered to stay away from you. I can't …" She shook her head. "I can't tell you more. I'm sorry."

The man on the street?

"This is about the man he stabbed? That man was trying to abduct me. He was attacking me!" I was hysterical and realized I was screaming.

"Not that one. They don't even know about that!" Than shouted from the porch while both men held him there. "The fucker you were enga—"

Forge's hand slapped over his mouth, stopping whatever else he was about to say.

He was going to say *engaged*. This … this was about Arden. I said nothing as I worked through that in my head. What did Arden have to do with this?

"He shouldn't have said that," she said. "Don't repeat it. That information could get you killed."

Get me killed …

"I don't understand," I told her. "Arden was my fiancé, but he left town. What does any of this have to do with him? Someone has the wrong information," I said vehemently.

Whoever had Ransom needed to know that. I had to tell them.

"No," she said softly, "they don't."

Yes! They did! Why wasn't she listening to me? I had to tell Linc. Go to Ocala. Someone had to stop them. They didn't understand.

"I know what happened!" I said, jabbing a finger into my chest. "I have to tell them! Whatever they think, they're wrong! Help me. Who do I call? Where do I go?" I asked, then sobbed again.

They had to listen to me. Ransom was in trouble, and Than was right. It was all my fault.

Spinning around, I barely had time to grab my hair before the first heave. The coffee I had drunk in the hotel room was all there was in my stomach to expel. Acid burned my throat, and another wave hit me. My chest constricted, and the hot tears continued to course down my face.

I had to save him. I had to get to him.

A hand touched my back gently. I knew it had to be Branwen. If Than had gotten free, he'd have me on the ground, choking the life out of me. And I would let him without a fight.

"He didn't do anything," I sobbed out, wrapping my arms around my waist as I stood back up.

"Yes," she whispered, "he did. And he admitted it."

I blinked as I stared out into the parking lot. What? No, Arden had left me a note. Ransom hadn't done anything.

"Why would he take the blame?" I asked hoarsely.

Branwen's hand fell from my back, but she didn't move away. "Arden's parents sent a PI." Her words were so quiet that I wouldn't have been able to hear her if I wasn't standing so close. She didn't want the men to know she was telling me anything. "He knew things. It caused issues that had to be cleaned up." I heard her swallow hard. "Linc begged him to stay away from you or he'd end up—" She stopped. But I knew. She was going to say *dead*.

I couldn't live in a world where he didn't exist.

"What is it they think he did?" I asked helplessly.

"He got rid of your fiancé."

This wasn't real. This had to be a nightmare. Things like this didn't happen in real life.

"Arden left a note and disappeared before anything started between Ransom and me. I mean, other than our texting and that first time he showed up at my apartment. We had only been on friendly terms."

I started to turn around and look at her, but her hand was on my back again.

"Don't," she hissed. "Bend over again like you need to throw up more."

I hesitated, then did as she'd said. Out of all the people here, I decided trusting her was my best option.

"Ransom's feelings for you ran deeper much sooner than he let on. He is guilty. Can you live with that?" she asked hesitantly. "Knowing what he is capable of?"

The ground came and went out of focus as I kept my eyes on the vomit that was splattered at my feet.

"They do things that most can't fathom. Their moral code is measured by a different set of standards. Loving one of them isn't for the weak. And that love has to be all-consuming."

Organized crime. The Southern Mafia. I'd watched Ransom stab a man in the lungs and not care that he was struggling to breathe. He let him die. That hadn't been his first kill. Could I live with that?

There wasn't even guilt as I replied, "I can't live without him. If he … if he—" I fought against the sob. "I can live with anything as long as he is alive."

I heard her let out a relieved sigh. "Okay, if that's the case, I have an idea."

I turned to look at her, forgetting I was supposed to be pretending I was still sick and not having a conversation with her. "What?" I asked, the tiniest bit of hope clinging to my sorrow.

"I'll tell you on the flight there. Let's go," she replied.

I didn't ask questions. Whatever I was told to do, I would do.

"What did you say to her?" Than demanded.

She stopped and put her hands on her hips as she stared up at the porch. "I know you're upset. I get it. You've already lost one brother, and the idea of losing another is more than you can handle. But right now, I need you to get it together. Noa wants to save Ransom, and I have a plan. But you have to calm down and help. It'll go a lot smoother."

Than's eyes darted between the two of us. "What can she do to help?" he asked, not sounding convinced.

"More than you can, acting like you're about to attack a woman," she snapped. "Forge, get a plane ready at the airstrip. Gathe, stay here and lock things up."

"Where do I tell the pilot we are going?" Forge asked.

"Ocala," she replied.

"You're taking her to Ocala?" Than asked with disbelief in his tone.

"Yes. And if any of you alert Linc before we arrive, then you'll have to deal with me. Be warned, I've gotten real damn good at target practice."

"What can she do?" Than demanded.

Branwen cut her eyes back to him. "She can appeal to the one woman with the power to control Blaise Hughes."

They all stilled and stared at her.

"Y-you're taking her to talk to Madeline Hughes?" Than asked.

"I sure as hell am. Now, are you going to shut up and do as I said or stand there and stare at me like I've lost my mind?"

"I'm coming with you," Than told her.

"Which is why Gathe is locking up," she replied, then snapped her fingers. "Let's get going, boys."

"Linc may kill all three of us for letting you do this," Forge said.

"Linc won't be killing anyone. Not if he wants in my bed again."

179

She turned back to me. "You still up for this?"

I nodded. "Yes. I'll do anything. But who is Madeline Hughes?" Not that it mattered.

The corners of her mouth quirked. "The boss's wife."

TWENTY-FIVE
NOA

There was more silence on the flight than I'd expected, but it gave me time to think. The uncertainty of what I was about to do was clear, even if they weren't saying it. I could feel the tension in the air. A mixture of fear, anxiety, and determination.

The little Branwen had made it clear she trusted Madeline Hughes, but the two men with us didn't seem so sure.

Than had only stopped pacing to sit down for takeoff. Once we were in the air, he was back to his feet, unable to stop moving. He was scared. Not for himself, but for Ransom. It was easy to read on his face.

A few times, he stopped. Once to place both his palms on the wall while he hung his head and took a few deep breaths. The other was to run both hands through his hair and fist it like he wanted to yank it out at the roots. He reminded me of a caged wild animal, and I understood that feeling completely.

I sat the entire flight, but I wrung my hands so much and so hard that they were raw and tender.

When we landed, there was a black SUV waiting on us, and Forge climbed into the driver's seat while Than got into the front passenger seat.

Again, no one said anything while we drove. My heart was hammering so hard in my chest that I wasn't so sure it would survive this without giving out on me. Like Than, it wasn't my life I was terrified of losing. Knowing that the outcome of this meeting meant life or ... no, I couldn't think about that. Ransom was going to grow old. He'd live a full, long life. Even if I didn't get to be a part of it. I had to know he was okay. Breathing. Living.

"Did you explain to her that he may kill all of us for this?" Than asked, breaking the silence.

"In so many words," Branwen replied with a hint of hesitance.

I glanced over at her. She hadn't told me that. I studied her, and she gave me an apologetic smile.

"I thought I was the only one putting their life on the line."

She lifted a shoulder. "Possibly. But with Blaise, one never knows."

Wait. She was serious.

"Branwen is safe. She's a Shephard, and Madeline would never forgive Blaise. It's the rest of us that are questionable." Forge supplied that information like it was normal conversation.

"Neither of you has to go. We can go alone," Branwen told them.

"Like hell. Dad wouldn't let me come, and that was fucked up. He's my brother," Than sneered.

"I helped bring you here. I wouldn't have done that if I had planned on walking away from it. We lost one brother. We don't want to lose another," Forge told her.

Branwen nodded and took a deep, steadying breath, then turned to look at me. "A few years ago, one of the guys was shot and killed. He was Than's best friend."

"Crosby," I said softly, remembering the day I'd gotten the text from Ransom about it.

She nodded slightly. "You know a lot."

"Ransom and I might have met in person again this past fall, but he's been a big part of my life for eleven years. We've shared most of our highs and lows with each other."

And I'd give it all up, everything we had, if he got to live.

"We only know a little about it. Ransom didn't share much," she told me.

"Has he really been talking to you since high school?" Than asked, his voice not hiding the disbelief.

"Texting," I supplied.

"How often?"

"It varied. It could be several times a day or a few times a week. Our lives would get busy. There was no pattern to it."

"It was you," he muttered. "Fucker was texting you."

I looked at the back of his head, waiting for him to say more.

Forge glanced over at him. "The times he was weird with his phone?"

"Yeah."

Forge's eyes shot up to the rearview mirror and met mine before dropping back to the road.

"Here," Branwen instructed, leaning forward. "Madeline said she'd be parked in a pearl-colored G-Wagon around the side of the store."

Forge frowned. "You're meeting her at a spa?"

"Yep."

"Damn, she's sharp," Than said.

183

Forge smirked. "The trackers," he said, as if understanding. "She told him she was going to the spa."

"There," Than said, pointing at the vehicle we were looking for.

Forge pulled up on the other side of it so that we were blocked from the view of the road and rest of the parking lot.

Branwen reached over to cover my clasped hands with one of hers and squeezed reassuringly. "Ready?"

I nodded.

The vehicle came to a stop, and I unbuckled and reached for the door handle.

"I can't lose him," Than said thickly.

I turned my gaze toward him. "Me neither," I replied, then took one more deep breath and stepped out of the SUV into the bright Florida sunshine.

Although I'd replayed what I'd say to Madeline Hughes hundreds of times in my head since we'd left Madison, the pressure that was riding on this conversation made me feel unprepared.

The windows to the Mercedes G-Wagon were so darkly tinted that I couldn't see who was inside. The driver's door opened as we approached, and a man stepped out, dressed in jeans, boots, and a fitted black T-shirt. He was tall with dark hair, almost black, and when he reached up and took off his sunglasses, a pair of blue-gray eyes stared back at me. As if sizing me up.

"Hello, Trev," Branwen said.

He turned his gaze to hers and smiled. "Good to see you, Branwen."

"Are you the only one with her?"

A smirk touched his lips, and his eyes twinkled with what looked like mischief. "I'm the only one the bastard won't kill over this."

Had he just called Blaise Hughes a bastard?

"Noa, this is Trev Hughes," Branwen told me.

He flashed a smile. "The younger brother."

Oh. I hadn't realized there were two sons. Perhaps they had two for backup. A spare. Like royalty.

Trev's eyes did a scan of the area. Then he opened the back door and waved a hand for us to get inside.

Branwen stepped forward and went in first.

Although there was a cool breeze, there was a trickle of sweat rolling down my back. I glanced up at Trev Hughes before following her inside.

"If anyone can free him, she can," he told me. "Relax. He's alive. I saw him myself this morning."

A sob slipped out of me at his words, and I covered my mouth as relief hit me so hard that I lost my breath.

His gaze softened, and he nodded his head for me to get inside. "Better hurry. The fucker is hard to fool. He's always one step ahead."

By *he*, I assumed that he was talking about Blaise.

With that warning, I climbed in quickly.

Sitting in the seat, I expected to see Branwen in the captain's chair opposite of me. Instead, it was a gorgeous woman with flawless features and platinum-blonde hair, slicked back in a low ponytail, wearing a diamond on her finger that could be used as a signal to land a plane.

"I'll start by telling you up front that I'm a fan, and although I would have met with you at Branwen's request, I'm going to use it as a bargaining chip for an early copy of the next book. Signed, of course," she said with a smile on her lips.

I blinked, staring at her. She was serious. I wasn't sure at first, but the slightly amused challenge in her eyes told me she meant it.

"I don't know much. Blaise doesn't involve me in the workings of the business unless it is horse-related. What is it you need from me? I don't mean to rush you, but my husband has a track record of knowing when I am disobeying him. Since I chose Trev to be my driver to the spa, there is a chance Blaise will question my motives. We could have been followed. Talk quick."

I nodded, feeling the pressure return. The desperate need to save Ransom. Say whatever I needed to in order to have this woman help me. If she truly did have that power over her husband. I hoped Branwen was right.

"He has Ransom, my … my—"

"Ransom Carver and Noa are in love. Well, she is in love with him, and he was willing to face death in order to be with her," Branwen explained.

"And I didn't know. He didn't tell me. He … he did something that I don't have the details to and was in trouble about it. He wasn't supposed to see me. I thought he was just done with me. But he showed up on New Year's Eve in New York. Said he loved me." My eyes filled with tears. "That he wanted forever. Then … then he was gone."

Madeline turned her gaze back to Branwen. "Blaise ordered him to stay away from her?"

She nodded. "Yes. He did something with her fiancé. That's all I know from the little I tried to listen in on. It caused issues. A PI showed up in Madison. Ransom was forbidden to see Noa after that. But he didn't listen."

"And Ransom is in Ocala? Blaise has him?"

Branwen nodded, her expression grim.

Madeline turned back to me. "Knock on that window twice, would you?"

I shifted in my seat to do as she'd said.

186

The door immediately opened, and Trev Hughes leaned inside. "You rang."

"Why does Blaise have Ransom Carver?" she asked matter-of-factly.

Trev laid his arm over the top of the door, facing us as he appeared to get comfortable. "He handed a man over to the cartel to get rid of him. The man's parents didn't let it rest, and his attempt to cover his trail failed. PI started digging around. Found out shit he isn't supposed to know. That had to be cleaned up. Ransom had acted on his own and without permission. Blaise sent word that he was to stay away from this one." He cut his eyes at me. "His visits to her had been documented by the PI. It's how he found the link to Ransom and dug into the family. But Ransom didn't stay away. He got a burner phone, put cameras in her apartment, had trackers on her, and watched her every move. Made nighttime trips to Manhattan more than once on a private plane. Blaise sent Gage to get him when the tracker that had been placed on his burner phone showed that he'd once again taken off to NYC on New Year's Eve. Gage brought him back here, strung him up underground, and his fate is still being discussed."

I'd just learned several things about Ransom. Things that should have horrified me. Starting with the fact that he was truly behind Arden's disappearance. He had cameras in my apartment. He watched me. He tracked me. There was a darkness I hadn't known existed in him. He'd warned me, but I'd never imagined that it was that twisted. Void of morals.

"Now, you've heard it all," Madeline said. "You know exactly what Ransom is. Who he is. What this life is."

I said nothing as I stared at her. The fear that she wouldn't believe he was worth saving began to sink in, and panic shoved all other thoughts aside. How would I convince her? What if this was it? I'd failed.

"Do you still want me to save him?"

My nails cut into my palms, as I fisted them so tightly. "I don't want to live in a world where he isn't." And that was my truth. The mark on my soul.

I loved Ransom Carver unconditionally. That wasn't going to change.

She smiled then and nodded her head at Trev, and the door clicked shut behind me.

"Right answer," she replied, then reached for her seat belt. "Buckle up. This car will ding at us until all the seat belts are fastened."

My gaze swung from her to Branwen, who was already reaching for her buckle. We were riding with her? I'd assumed we would get back in the SUV we had come in.

"Where are we going?" I asked as Trev climbed back into the driver's seat.

Madeline crossed her legs and leaned back. "Going to get your man."

TWENTY-SIX
THAN

There wasn't even a name that I could give to the fucking twisted shit that had been going on inside me since I'd been told that my brother had been taken to Ocala. Losing my best friend, watching Crosby die right in front of me, the light leave his eyes, it had marked me in a way I would never get over. I still had nightmares, reliving it. Seeing him stare up at me. Whisper Halo's name. Trying to tell me something I hadn't understood back then.

But my brother? I'd not recover from it. If Blaise Hughes took his life, I was done. They could hunt me down and string me up too. I didn't fucking care. I couldn't lose Ransom.

Which was why I was following a nice older lady by the name of Ms. Jimmie to Blaise Hughes's office, uninvited. Why Forge was beside me I didn't know. He hadn't been forced to come inside with me. Hell, I hadn't even asked him to. When I'd gotten out of the SUV and started for the house, he had followed.

Ms. Jimmie smiled at us as she stopped in front of the door to Blaise's office. "I'll leave you here then," she replied before she walked back in the direction she had come.

She hadn't knocked or asked if we could come in. That should be a warning right there. Not even the damn housekeeper would interrupt him without invitation to.

I stared at the imposing dark mahogany door. "You don't have to go in there," I said.

"Yeah," Forge replied, "I do."

Shaking my head, I tried again to change his mind. "No reason for both of us to put our lives on the line."

Forge didn't move.

I cut my eyes at him. "You know how risky this is. What if Noa's attempt doesn't work?"

We'd left her there in the G-Wagon with Madeline Hughes. Both her and Branwen. Not waiting for the outcome. I didn't trust that a woman could convince Blaise Hughes of anything. Even his wife. The man was known far and wide for his ruthlessness. Most called him the Devil and believed it.

"If it was Oz's life, would you stand back and let me go in alone?" he asked, finally meeting my gaze.

No. I wouldn't. We weren't all related, but the ties of family ran deep. We'd been raised as family. Trained as brothers. Even in this life that I sometimes wished I could walk away from, I never wanted to walk away from them. I wasn't fighting for a break from the darkness anymore. I'd found my peace, my solace, my center. Montana had become all that for me. She was what I had been missing in life.

As fucking angry as I was at Noa Raines because I needed to take my pain out on someone, if she was that for my brother, then I understood every-fucking-thing he'd done in order to have her.

He didn't deserve to die for it.

"All right then," I replied with a nod, then lifted my hand to knock. Just opening the door and walking inside could get us both shot before we took the first step. I had some things to say before that happened.

I heard the rumble of deep voices inside. My dad was probably in there. I didn't allow myself to think about his reaction to my showing up here. He'd looked so fucking stricken when Linc told him that Blaise had sent Gage Presley to take Ransom out of a hotel room in Manhattan, where he'd been with Noa. He wouldn't like this. It would scare the shit out of him. Mom had fought hard to keep Ransom and me out of this life when we were kids. It was the end to their marriage. But we'd chosen Dad and the family. It had broken her heart, and although we still visited her and called, she wasn't a part of our world. Not really.

For reasons like this one right now. What she had always feared the most. Losing one of us.

The doorknob turned, and Levi Shephard opened the door. His eyes went from Forge, then locked on mine. I could see the displeasure in his eyes.

The silent *What the fuck are you doing?* was clear even if he didn't say a word to us.

He turned back to the room of men. "Than and Forge," he said, but nothing more.

I heard my father's curse and a heavy sigh, which I assumed came from Linc. Jonas—Forge's dad—wasn't in there. He'd stayed in Madison to oversee things there, along with Oz, Locke, and Fender.

Levi turned back to us. "Fucking stupid," he muttered under his breath as he stepped back for us to enter. He was referring to the two of us. That didn't bode well for us.

191

Levi was one of Blaise's men. The ones who worked close to him. That he'd once lived with. There were many Shephards inside the family in more than one state. All descendants from Jediah Hughes's best friend, Charles Shephard. However, Levi had been raised in Ocala with Blaise. Linc and Garrett—Blaise's father—had also grown up together, and before moving to Mississippi to take over things, Linc had always lived here.

But we weren't dealing with Garrett. He had handed over the reins to Blaise to enjoy his life with his new wife. Blaise lacked the charm and charisma that Garrett had been known for. And connections to his ancestors didn't seem to be of concern to him. He demanded obedience. Ransom hadn't obeyed.

If only Trev Hughes had been the firstborn, things would be so much easier.

I stepped in front of Forge and entered the room. My gaze instantly found my father, who was standing in the center of the room, looking pale and livid.

Sorry, Pop. But it's Ransom. I had to do something.

"Don't tell us," Luther Levine drawled from the other side of the room. "You two were in the neighborhood and thought you'd stop by for a slice of pie."

I glanced over at Luther to see him sitting on a high-back leather chair with a cigar between his teeth and a glass of whiskey balanced on his knee. He gave me a shake of his head, like he thought I was a fool, but said nothing more.

"You need to leave, son," my father said between clenched teeth.

"Let me guess. Jonas and Oz don't know you flew the coop either, do they?" Luther asked Forge, but I didn't take my gaze from my father's.

"They're here now, Hale," Linc interjected in a hard tone that was a warning for my father not to make a scene. To back down.

Dad's breathing was heavy enough that his shoulders rose and fell visibly. He was terrified.

"Sorry," I said simply. And I was sorry that I'd just added to the stress and fear he was already under. But I wasn't sorry that I had come to try and do something to save my brother.

"Who else is here?" Linc asked me.

I wasn't about to tell him Branwen had come with us, along with Noa. He was likely to gun us both down right here. Although it had been his wife's plan.

"Just us," I replied, looking from my father to Linc.

Although I hadn't made eye contact with Blaise Hughes, I felt his stare. The force of it could be felt throughout the room. Like a warning or an omen of evil.

"Seems your boys have a problem with obedience, Hale."

The deep voice sent a shiver down my spine, but I didn't allow it to show in my expression. I shifted my eyes to the desk in the center of the room, where Blaise Hughes sat. His elbows on the table, a glass of whiskey in one hand, and a merciless gleam in his green eyes as he watched me like a lion would his prey.

"He didn't beat 'em enough," Luther said.

"I'm sorry, Blaise," my father told him.

Blaise didn't acknowledge his words as he flickered his gaze from me to Forge. "And you're here because?" he asked him.

"Ransom is family. He's my brother too," was his simple response. His voice didn't waver, and I was fucking proud of that.

"Jesus Christ," Linc hissed in frustration.

193

If he wasn't ready to hand the branch over to Bane before now, he might be once this was over. We weren't ready for that though. Bane was still one of us. Too young to be in charge. Not that we'd have any say in it. When the time came, the man currently behind the desk would make the call.

The silence that followed was eerie. Especially in a room full of men. I hadn't scanned the place or checked out everyone in attendance, but I'd seen enough from my peripheral vision to know who lined the walls. Blaise's men were all here, but one from what I could see. Huck would be hard to miss in a room. He'd take up enough of it, so his absence was easy to note.

Other than Levi, who had taken position on the back right wall, behind Blaise, there was Kye—Luther's son—standing to his back left. I'd only seen a glimpse of him, but Gage was behind me, in the right corner of the room, sitting on the edge of a table with a cigarette in his mouth, flicking a lighter in his hand. His silence was possibly more intimidating than anything else. He didn't have the power Blaise wielded, but he was insane. Unpredictable. And that made him someone you wanted to steer clear of.

The main branch of the family had more men, but everyone knew that those four were his closest friends. The ones he trusted the most. His brother didn't count because he was a Hughes. He was also nothing like Blaise and held more of their father's charm. Possibly all of it.

"If no one is gonna ask"—a sadistic chuckle came from the back corner behind me—"I gotta know. What is it that you two thought you could do, showing up here?"

Blaise's eyes cut to where I knew Gage was sitting. He didn't smile or even change his expression in the least.

"What? I'm curious?" Gage said.

Blaise ignored him, and his eyes moved back to mine just as another knock on the door echoed through the room.

"I swear to God, that'd better not be another one of you," Linc snarled.

It wasn't. I shook my head once at him to assure him that I'd not lied.

Blaise's expression took on a lethal quality that made my blood run cold. "See who it is," he said to Gage.

I heard him stand, but didn't turn to watch what was about to happen next. There was a good chance that was Madeline Hughes. If she had decided to grant Noa's request, then we might all die. I couldn't imagine the man glowering this way to be forgiving about bringing his wife into the situation. Branwen had believed differently though. We could only hope she was right.

"I don't need an introduction, Gage," a female voice said with no trace of fear, followed by the click of high heels on the hardwood floor as she entered the room.

"Madeline," Blaise said sharply, his gaze locked on the woman behind me. "Are the boys okay?" he asked, standing up.

"The boys are fine," she said as she passed by my right side and went to stand slightly in front of Forge and me.

The blonde was my age, but had been with Blaise since she had been nineteen years old. She didn't cower or appear at all concerned with the severe expression on his face. Instead, she stood with her back straight and a defiant tilt of her chin and stared him down.

"We need to talk," she told him.

"Can it wait until after this is finished?" he asked.

"No. It's about this," she said with a wave of her hand as she glanced around the room. She paused when she saw Linc and waved with a wiggle of her fingers and a bright smile, then turned back to her husband.

Blaise hadn't sat back down. Narrowing his eyes at her, he crossed his arms over his chest, as if waiting for her to continue.

"It's probably best we spoke alone," she told him.

He studied her for a moment before speaking again. "Madeline, this isn't a concern of yours. It's family business. You don't even know what we are meeting about."

She glared at him. Holy shit. I held my breath.

"Yes, honey, I do know what it is about. I've had the CliffsNotes version at least. And I have some issues with it that need to be discussed … now."

Damn. She had balls.

The entire room was so silent that I was guessing everyone was holding their breath. No one spoke to Blaise like that. If they did, they hadn't lived to tell the tale.

His hands dropped as he started around the desk, the displeasure in his eyes darkening as he closed the distance between them. A larger, dangerous man would have cowered at this point. But the blonde smokeshow did not. She actually raised an eyebrow in challenge.

"Madeline." He said her name as if scolding a child.

"We can do this here. Or we can do it in private," she told him, not even shifting one fucking inch back.

His nostrils flared as he towered over her. She tilted her head back and met his glare with one of her own. The tension in the room was so thick that not even Luther was making one of his smart-ass quips.

"Tell me why you're in here," he said in a low, deep voice.

"To stop you from killing a man who you commanded to stay away from the woman he loves," she shot back at him without pause. "Now, would you like to speak in private?"

His eyes flared hotly, and I began to fear for Branwen's life, along with my brother's. Hell, we all might be wiped out. Every member of the Mississippi branch that was here.

"Who told you that?" he asked.

"Does it matter?" she shot back at him.

"I need to know who dies next."

Fuck.

She laughed. A soft musical sound that did not fit with this moment. "You won't kill Trev."

Blaise's jaw ticced, and I wasn't so sure his brother was safe this time.

"This isn't your business. You need to leave and go tell my brother he'd better go hide behind our father's coattails." Blaise started to walk back around his desk as if the conversation was over.

"I won't allow you to kill Ransom Carver," Madeline said with a hint of defiance in her tone.

Blaise stilled then and turned back around slowly to look at his wife.

"I won't, and don't look at me like that. I told you we could do this in private," she snapped.

"You don't know the situation, and you don't tell me what I am and am not going to do."

She placed her manicured hands on her hips and cocked her head slightly. "I do know the situation. I know that Ransom is family. And he didn't do anything directly to you. He didn't try to maliciously defy you. His actions had nothing to do with you or the family," she said, raising her voice and closing the space he'd put between them. "In fact, he stood in front of you at the Derby after-party when the first shot was fired. He was ready to take a bullet for you."

"He did." Luther's voice surprised me. I glanced over at him as he took a sip of his whiskey. "Take a bullet that night, that is."

"Thank you, Luther," Madeline said before Blaise could respond. "See, he is loyal. But you were demanding he stay away from the woman he is in love with. And he tried. She thought he'd ghosted her. He broke her heart, and all because he was trying to obey you."

Blaise's gaze didn't soften. In fact, it might have gotten more chilling.

"Trev tell you all that too?" he asked.

She rolled her eyes.

"I asked you a question, Madeline. How do you know how Noa Raines was affected?"

When she didn't respond, I wondered if this was the point where she cowered. I glanced over at my father, who was watching the two of them. His eyes shot to meet mine, and I could see the question in them and the trace of hope.

"Because I've spoken to her."

Here we go.

I looked at Forge hesitantly as we waited for what was to come next. He was as fucking tense as I was.

"When did you speak to Noa Raines?" Blaise demanded.

"An hour ago."

"Where?"

"Inside my G-Wagon, in the parking lot of the spa."

"On the phone?" he asked.

"No."

His eyes flared. "She was in your vehicle with you?"

"Yes, she was. Along with Branwen," Madeline said matter-of-factly.

"Oh shit," Luther muttered. "Someone, pass the popcorn."

Blaise's gaze shot to Linc, and I couldn't even look over at him. I stared at the ground instead.

"Don't you glare at Linc! He did nothing wrong. Branwen is my friend. She wanted to meet with me and introduce me to my favorite romance author. Just so happens you were trying to kill the man she loves because he would rather die than be away from her," Madeline said.

Blaise's arm shot out and pointed to the door. "Outside," he said, raising his voice.

"Not unless you're coming with me."

"I. Am," he said through clenched teeth.

She lifted one shoulder in a shrug. "I did try and have this conversation in private. You were the one who refused to—"

"Madeline!" he shouted, stopping her from whatever else she was about to say.

"Do not yell at me, Blaise Hughes," she warned him.

His hand wrapped around her upper arm, and he took her with him as he stalked toward the door. No one spoke. I wasn't sure hearts were even beating at this point. We were all frozen as we watched them leave. The door slamming behind them.

No one moved. My eyes flickered over to Forge, who had paled slightly—but then I probably had too. I still didn't chance a look in Linc's direction.

"Well, didn't this just take a fun turn?" Luther said.

"Dad," Kye said sharply, speaking for the first time.

"What? It did," he said with a smirk, then took another drink from his glass.

"You brought Branwen here?" The underlying fury in Linc's tone was expected.

"Branwen is a grown woman, Linc," Luther interjected. "Those two didn't bring her anywhere."

"What the fuck were you both thinking?" Linc demanded angrily.

I lifted my chin and met his furious glare. "That I would do anything to save my brother."

"We were handling things," my father said.

Cutting my eyes from Linc to him, I asked, "And how was that working out? Where is Ransom? Not in here, is he?"

"You don't bring the women into this," Dad said.

"I didn't. She brought herself. Noa showed up at the distillery, looking for Ransom. When she found out he was taken here, she got so upset that she started puking. Branwen went down to talk to her, and before we knew it, Branwen was ordering Forge to call for a plane, and we were all headed here."

A deep chuckle came from Luther. "Ah damn. I love that woman."

Linc took several deep breaths, and his eyes shot to the closed door. His anger had morphed into panic.

"Branwen will be fine," Levi told his father. "The only person on earth who can make Blaise do their bidding is Madeline. Trev, however, may need to go to Garrett's until Blaise cools down."

TWENTY-SEVEN
RANSOM

The feeling in my arms was taking a while to return. I shook them a little as I sat down on a stool across the bar from Huck, who was getting down a bottle of whiskey from the shelf. He'd come to get me from the underground, but said little else. I'd be relieved, but this didn't mean forgiveness or freedom. For all I knew, I was being allowed one last drink before the end came.

"How long was I down there?" I asked, not even sure what day it was.

"Thirty hours, give or take," he replied, placing a glass in front of me, then lifting a bottle of our best label to fill my glass.

I needed water. A lot of it, but I wasn't going to complain. If this was my last hour, then I'd rather end it with my grandfather's recipe.

I picked up the glass and started to down it, but decided to take it slow. Stretch this out a little longer.

"You gonna tell me why I'm here?" I asked. "In the game room of Garrett's house, that is and not still strung up."

Huck poured his own glass. "Blaise don't like to take business around the boys and Maddy."

Man of many words. That didn't answer my question. I didn't give a fuck whose house I was at. I wanted to know why I wasn't still tied up.

"Not what I'm asking," I told him.

He smirked and took a drink as he lifted his eyes to mine. "I know."

Bastard.

Maybe I didn't need to be aware of what was to come. Going in blindly might be best.

I took a long drink, forgetting my decision to go slowly. I was thirsty. When I set it back down, I figured I might as well ask what I wanted. It wasn't like anything I said would change the outcome.

"Think he'd let me call Noa?" I asked, my chest constricting as I thought about her face. "Before …" I added. Not finishing that sentence.

Huck shrugged and leaned to rest his hip on the edge of the counter as he crossed one arm over his chest and held his glass with the other. "No reason to."

His nonchalance sent rage coursing through me, and I fought to tamp it down. I wasn't in a position to lose my fucking shit on anyone. If there was a shred of hope I might live, I didn't want to chance anything.

The door to the room opened behind me, and I turned to see Blaise Hughes enter alone. Dread replaced the hope at the glint in his eyes as they leveled on me. Not what I'd call promising. I'd been visited by Huck, Gage, and Levi. But this was the first time seeing Blaise since my arrival.

His gaze cut to Huck's, and he nodded once. Huck turned and got down another glass. He said nothing as he approached and jerked out the stool two seats over from me with more force than necessary before sitting down.

Huck slid the almost-full glass of bourbon over to him, and he took it, tossing it back in one long gulp. When he put it back on the bar, Huck lifted the bottle and poured him some more.

Blaise cut his eyes to me then. "I've killed men for less," he said. "Defiance is something I don't overlook."

I said nothing. He didn't want my explanation. If he had, he'd have asked me by now.

"I don't like killing family. It weakens the power, puts a crack in the loyalty," he said, then took a normal drink from his glass this time. "Overlooking disobedience, however, also weakens the power."

If he wanted me to respond, I had nothing to say. At least that he wanted to hear. In my opinion, his command for me to stay away from someone I needed to survive this life was what had fucking weakened his power. He had my loyalty. He had all our loyalty. But he loved a woman. He should understand that it was its own brand of loyalty. One that trumped everything else.

"Linc Shephard fucking babysat me as a kid. Levi is as close as a brother to me as Trev. Having Linc in my office, doing his best to convince me that you should live, put me in a position I didn't like. But I had been trained not to allow my emotions make my decisions." He picked up his glass again and stared at it before taking a long drink.

I continued to wait. I still had no idea what my outcome would be, but I wished he'd just tell me already.

"Doesn't matter now though," he said with a humorless chuckle. "My wife stepped in. She took the decision out of my hands."

What? I glanced at Huck—who might be almost smirking, but I wasn't sure—then back to Blaise.

He turned his head to look at me. "You put your life on the line for the love of a woman. Disobeyed a direct order because you couldn't let her go," he said, then shoved the stool back as he stood up again. "Count yourself lucky that my wife got in your corner. Because it's the love I have for that woman that I'm not doing something I didn't want to fucking do anyway. At the rate the Mississippi branch was showing up on my land, there would have likely been a goddamn war if I'd killed your ass for defying my orders."

He gave Huck an annoyed glance, then turned and started back toward the door he'd come in through.

What the hell had just happened? I didn't know Madeline that well. What did she have to do with this? Not that I wasn't eternally grateful, but seriously, what the fuck?

"Can you tell her thank you for me?" I asked his retreating form.

He nodded, but didn't look back.

I chanced one more question. "Why did she do it?"

He paused at the doorway and glanced over his shoulder. "For a signed advanced copy of Juliette Romeo's next book." The hint of a grin played across his normally severe expression before he walked away.

I stared at the empty space where he had been as his words registered and made sense in my head.

Noa.

But ... how?

"She's got a set on her," Huck said, and I swung my eyes over to see him watching me.

"Who?" I asked, not sure if he was talking about Madeline or Noa.

"Your woman," he said, shoving off from where he'd been leaning.

"Noa …" I said.

He cocked an eyebrow. "You got more than one? I wouldn't tell her that if you do."

I shook my head, standing up as my mind raced. How did Huck know Noa? Was she here?

"No! Of course not. Where is she?" I asked.

"Waiting on you. She wouldn't go to the airstrip without you. Everyone else has already headed that way. Don't think she trusts us much."

She was here. My heart took off at a full gallop, and I started for the door.

Noa had come to Ocala. How did she even know where I was? Jesus Christ, what had she been thinking? Blaise could have reacted badly to her arrival.

"She's waiting outside in the Escalade!" Huck called out, and I broke into a run.

TWENTY-EIGHT

NOA

When the second one of the massive double doors to the house opened, I took a step in that direction. I'd been out here for over thirty minutes, waiting on Ransom. Branwen had convinced Linc to let me stay. Even if she hadn't, no one would have gotten me to budge. I wasn't going until I had Ransom by my side.

He came barreling outside, and my heart leaped in my chest as my eyes filled with water. Relief rushed over me as I began walking in his direction. His eyes lasered in on me as he made his way down the elaborate steps leading up to the Hughes's mansion.

His long strides turned into a jog, and joy from the sight of him bubbled out of me in a teary laugh. When he closed the last few feet between us, he grabbed my face with both hands and slammed his mouth down over mine. I clung to his arms, pressing into him. He was alive. He was here.

Our tongues tangled in their own desperation, and my tears wet both our cheeks before he broke the kiss and stared down at me as he continued to cradle my face.

"What did you do?" he asked huskily.

I smiled and sniffled up at him. "Came to bring you home."

He closed his eyes briefly, and his body trembled slightly before he opened them again. "Do you have any idea how dangerous this was?"

I nodded. "Yes."

"And you came anyway."

"You promised me forever."

He let out a disbelieving laugh. "Yeah, I did," he agreed, tucking a strand of hair behind my ear. His gaze seemed to devour me, as if the sight of me made everything else fade away. "How did you do it?" he asked. "Am I really getting to live because of a signed book?"

I lifted a shoulder, trying my best to be nonchalant. "I have my own set of strengths. You have your guns, and I have my words. Mine is a much more humane, civilized way to handle a situation."

He leaned down and kissed me gently again before whispering against my lips, "I love you."

"I love you too."

"I'm ready for that forever. Tell me you'll leave Manhattan and come back home."

I smiled. Once, I'd have balked if someone had called Madison home. I'd never felt at home there. But my home wasn't a place. It was a person. And he was in Madison. His job required he live there. With mine, I could live anywhere.

"On one condition," I said.

He leaned back so he could look at my face. This was something we would have to discuss fully eventually.

"Anything," he replied.

ABBI GLINES

He said that now, but I had a feeling that he'd need a reminder of that in the future.

"Find a way to get Arden back from the cartel without getting killed."

The way his eyes flashed with shock told me he hadn't planned to ever tell me about how Arden had disappeared. I could hold it against him or accept it for who he was. After almost losing him, I found that I could forgive him his lack of morals.

"You know."

I nodded. "Yes, I do. And the video cameras in my apartment—I'm going to want to know exactly what all you saw. Did I dance naked around the house at any time? Because now that you are here and alive, I'm able to think about other things, and I do not like the things I am thinking. That's an invasion of privacy and—"

He stopped me with another kiss, and I slapped at his chest, which only made him chuckle.

"You put every stripper I've ever seen to shame with your moves, baby," he whispered with amusement.

My entire face flushed, and I closed my eyes tightly as the embarrassment sank in. I hadn't done it many times since the majority of the time, I was depressed from the shattering I'd gone through when I thought he'd tossed me aside. But even him seeing it once was humiliating.

He kissed both my heated cheeks. "It was the sexiest damn thing I've ever seen," he said in a husky voice.

"Hey! Can I drive?" a voice called out. "Or, hell, even ride in the back? Just get me off this property."

I looked around Ransom to see Trev Hughes jogging our way from the direction of the horse stables.

"You can drive," Ransom told him.

208

"Thanks! But we need to go now. You might not be getting smoked today, but I will be if he finds me."

Ransom put his arm around my back and pulled me against his side as Trev ran past us and jerked open the driver's door to climb inside.

"Guess he pissed off his brother," Ransom said with a shrug.

And I knew exactly how he had done it.

Ransom opened the back door and held my hand to help me inside. Glancing down, I saw the broken, raw skin around his wrists and let out a horrified gasp. Reaching down to gently take his hand, I looked back up at him.

"Your wrists," I said, feeling sick.

"Will heal. Get in, Shakespeare. I'm ready to get you home."

Home.

The one place I'd been searching for my entire life.

And I had finally found it.

Visit Abbiglinesbooks.com and join her VIP list for exclusive bonus scenes released monthly.

Do you love Luther Levine? Get ready for *Hell of a Mess* coming September 29, 2025. Can't wait? Then go sign up for Abbi's VIP list so you don't miss his prequel before his story releases.

ABOUT ABBI

Abbi Glines is a #1 New York Times, USA Today, Wall Street Journal, and International bestselling author of the Rosemary Beach, Sea Breeze, Smoke Series, Vincent Boys, Boys South of the Mason Dixon, and The Field Party Series. She is also author to the Sweet Trilogy and the Black Souls Trilogy. She believes in ghosts and has a habit of asking people if their house is haunted before she goes in it. Her house was built in 1820 and she finally has her own haunted house but they're friendly spirits. She drinks afternoon tea because she wants to be British but alas she was born in Alabama although she now lives in New England (which makes her feel a little closer to the British). When asked how many books she has written she has to stop and count on her fingers and even then she still forgets a few. When she's not locked away writing, she is entertaining her first grade daughter, she is reading (if everyone in her house including the ghosts will leave her alone long enough), shopping online (major Amazon Prime addiction), and planning her next Disney World vacation (and now that her oldest daughter Annabelle works at Disney she has an excuse to frequent it often).

You can connect with Abbi online in several different ways. She uses social media to procrastinate.

Facebook: AbbiGlinesAuthor
Twitter: abbiglines
Instagram: abbiglines
Snapchat: abbiglines
TikTok: abbiglines

.

Printed in Dunstable, United Kingdom

73355667R00138

First Impressions

first impressions

Linda Middleton

Choc Lit

A JOFFE BOOKS COMPANY

Choc Lit
A Joffe Books company
www.choc-lit.com

First published in Great Britain in 2024

© Linda Middleton 2024

Cover art by Lizzie Gardiner

ISBN: 978-1781897850